"For anyone who's heard about the incident of the boys trapped in the cave in Thailand in 2018, this book is like being there with them in the cave. Great and fast-paced read!"

—**Jamie Aagren**

I0549724

Praise for *Trapped in Thailand's Cave*

"I was glad to get out of the cave finally. The author is so knowledgeable about Thailand, scuba diving, caves, and Navy SEALs that only he could have written such an informed and remarkable book!"

—Marjorie Dixon Roxburgh

"I read it in one sitting and couldn't put it down! The author's stream of thought was so detailed and a delight. Lots of four-letter words flying around made it real. So touching about Buddhism—no desires and no expectations. Loved it!"

—Therese Araneta

"The first book written and published about Thailand's soccer boys—the Wild Boars. All the other books will finish behind Greenlaw."

—Supattra Manaban

"Great read on a totally different way of looking at the Wild Boars soccer team's venture into Tham Luang cave and their rescue. Obviously, the author understands Thai culture and their fascination with ghosts and the spirit world. I couldn't put it down even though I knew how the ending would turn out. What an imagination Raymond Greenlaw has! Loved it!"

—Glenn "Fiddlehead" Fleagle

"Incredibly creative and entertaining. The story has both a tragic and a happy ending."

—Anonymous Reviewer 1

"Brilliant. Riveting. Timely. Blending the facts of the incident at Tham Luang Cave in Chiang Rai, Thailand with the local legends of the cave, Greenlaw weaves a magnificent tale of the Wild Boars soccer team and what plausibly may have happened in the cave. He draws from all of his adventures and experience as an endurance athlete and world traveler to bring a unique and intimate perspective to this incredible story. Greenlaw's there as a fly on the wall."

—Peter Solomon

"I cried more than once at the predicament of the boys. Until I read Greenlaw's description, I hadn't thought through the plight of the boys in this way, to this extent: an amazing true story of the survival of a terrible ordeal. I won't be going in any caves again soon!"

—Anonymous Reviewer 2

"This book is a must read for anyone who followed the story of the soccer boys from Thailand."

—Wongduean Bohthong

"Meticulously researched. The author's attention to detail is marvelous. I felt like I was there."

—Paul Göransson

Trapped in Thailand's Cave

Trapped in Thailand's Cave

By
Raymond Greenlaw

Roxy Publishing, LLC
Savannah, Georgia
United States of America

Copy Editor—Marjorie Dixon Roxburgh
Cover Design—Robert Greenlaw
Text Design—Raymond Greenlaw
Typesetting—WORD – Garamond 12

Roxy Publishing
Savannah, Georgia 31419
United States of America

http://drraymondgreenlaw.com

First edition, paperback.

The publisher and the author do not advocate spelunking in Thailand during monsoon or any other
season, unless one is properly trained. Anyone cav-
ing does so voluntarily at his/her own risk realizing
that he/she may put the lives of others at great risk,
too. Please think twice before entering any cave.
You may be impacting the lives of others as well as
your own.

ISBN 978-1-947467-12-5 (paperback)

Dedication

To the Thai Navy SEAL
Lieutenant Commander Samarn Gunan.

Preface

This work of fiction is based on a true story. While cycling the remote Trans America Trail in June of 2018, I learned of a group of Thai boys who became trapped in the Tham Luang Cave in the northern Thai province of Chiang Rai. The boys are members of the Wild Boars soccer team from the Moo Pa Academy in Chiang Rai. Having visited numerous caves in Thailand myself and having spent many monsoon seasons in country, I could well understand the predicament of the boys. My 20+ years of scuba-diving experience, diving in cenotes and caves in the Yucatan, and my March trip this year to penetrate deeply into the wrecks of Chuuk Lagoon also helped me to grasp the extreme difficulty of a rescue and the urgency of the situation.

Unable to assist with the rescue efforts myself, I marveled at the bravery and courage of all of those involved: the rescuers and volunteers as well as the Wild Boars and their assistant coach. Tragically, the courageous Thai Navy SEAL, Samarn Gunan, died during the rescue mission. (Note that his last name is sometimes spelled Kunan or Poonan.) As a fellow endurance athlete and former professor, training partner, dive buddy, and mentor of future United States Navy SEALs at the United States Naval Academy in Annapolis, Maryland, I felt a deep respect for Samarn and tremendous sorrow for his family and friends. I've dedicated this book to him.

In Thailand most people believe in ghosts. Monks can be found throughout the country performing many types of ceremonies and rituals to protect people from ghosts and expel ghosts from unwanted places. I've attended many of these ceremonies. This novel tells a story about the ghosts of Tham Luang Cave in the Mountain of the Sleeping Lady and what happened to them in the cave during the time period June 23rd until July 6th in 2018, the period from when the Wild Boars and their assistant soccer coach became trapped in the cave until the day when Samarn Gunan died.

This tale intends no disrespect to Thai culture, local customs, legends, ghosts, accepted beliefs surrounding the Tham Luang Cave, any rescuers, volunteers, the Wild Boars soccer team and assistant coach, the Thai government, or anyone else involved with this incident. The plot follows local legend faithfully. I have only the deepest admiration and respect for all of those who were involved in the rescue efforts and the incident. The ghosts in this book express their opinions, but those aren't (necessarily) shared by the author. The narrating ghost, Uan, tells the story as he saw and thought that it unfolded. Any anachronism occurring in the book is intentional. The ghosts are well educated, Internet savvy, and supernatural.

Raymond Greenlaw

Since my completion of the Trans America Trail, I've been fascinated by the story of the Wild Boars and their assistant coach, as well as with the stories of all those brave, devoted, and giving individuals involved in the international rescue mission. From that fascination, from my personal experiences, from living in Thailand over a period of 15 years, and from my many trips to Chiang Rai, this work has emerged. A significant portion of the proceeds from this work will be used to support education in northern Thailand and the memory of Lieutenant Commander Gunan.

If you've been to Thailand or are familiar with the international rescue mission at Tham Luang Cave in 2018 in the Chiang Rai province, I hope that you find this book a valuable and interesting read. And, a book that remembers Samarn Gunan as a great Thai man, role model, and hero—pushing himself to the limit: mentally, physically, and spiritually—in the name of service to others. I am deeply saddened that I never had the chance to meet Lieutenant Commander Gunan.

Raymond Greenlaw
August 10, 2018

Acknowledgments

A special thanks to Wongduean "Kig" Bohthong for her support, suggestions, and cover design. Through many discussions with Kig, I was able to understand the situation at Tham Luang Cave much better and especially from the Thai point of view. She helped me to be sensitive to issues that would concern Thais surrounding the legend of the Mountain of the Sleeping Lady.

A special thanks to Marjorie Dixon Roxburgh for copy editing this manuscript. Her edits and corrections helped significantly to improve this work. Marjorie also helped in selecting the book's title and with the back cover copy. Although Marjorie is busy with her own writing projects, she set those aside for a period to assist me with this one. I greatly appreciate her effort and timeliness.

A warm thanks to Paul and Helen Göransson for their timely readings and comments on the manuscript. Their input helped to improve this book significantly.

A sincere thanks to all reviewers, both farangs and Thais, who provided me with constructive comments. Your suggestions have helped me to improve this book. I am indebted to you. Many others have contributed to this project, and a warm thanks goes to all of them.

Chapter 1

"Release the Wild Boars! Release the Wild Boars!" I screamed angrily.

My voice boomed through the dark Tham Luang Cave. As my echo dampened, I heard only the eerie, irregular pitter-patter of dripping water. No reply came. Flying around in a wild rage, I almost lost control. My back hit and broke off a small stalactite. Ouch!

Would my demand be enough? It needed to be for the sake of the Wild Boars soccer team and their assistant coach.

Who am I? My name is Uan. That's not my real name, of course, but like most Thai people, Thai ghosts in the underground assume a three-letter nickname. Oh, by the way, in the Thai language the word 'Uan' means fat. In the above-ground world, a Thai nickname given by a parent is used to conceal a child's true identity in an effort to protect the

Raymond Greenlaw   15

child from evil spirits. We simply carried that naming tradition into the spirit world even though we have no need to conceal our real identities in the underground. Nicknames are fun too. Maybe not in my case, but I was fat, so my nickname never bothered me that much.

There's no reason to tell you who I was above ground. Let's not go there. Just think of me as your humble narrator. I'll relate this story how *I* remember things transpiring in the Tham Luang Cave starting on June 23rd. I'll tell you what *I* heard and saw. If you'd been there, maybe *you* would have heard and seen things differently. I'll do my best, but if I botch a few of the details, please bear in mind the great stress that I was under at the time and my old age.

I lived in the Tham Luang Cave in Chiang Rai—the northernmost province of Thailand. I was trapped there many years ago. 'Tham Luang' means 'great cave,' and if you must be condemned to a cave, I suppose this one is great. The cave is inside Doi Nang Noi—the Mountain of the Sleeping Lady. Much more on her later. We lived up near Myanmar. Of course, when I first got confined to the cave, that country was called Mranma. Keep in mind this was long before the British changed the country's name to Burma. I'll spare you those details.

Earlier I said 'we.' That's right. I lived in the cave with my father (Kla), his younger brother

(Moo), my younger brother (Nid), and my older cousin (Ton). For those who don't speak Thai, let me translate: 'Kla' means brave, 'Moo' means pig, 'Nid' means small, and 'Ton' means leader. We had been enjoying our daily poker game on June 23, 2018 about a quarter mile from the cave's outer entrance when all hell broke loose. That fateful day, on which my story begins, changed the lives of the inhabitants and visitors of the Tham Luang Cave forever ...

"Are you in or not?" cousin Ton asked impolitely.

I looked at my cards again. I fidgeted. Pulling out one of the eights, I quickly inserted it back into my hand beside another eight. To stay in required another ten thousand.

"No, not with this hand I'm not. I've got nothin'," I said.

"Moo?" Ton inquired.

"I'm out too," Uncle Moo said.

Uncle Moo folded. His white face showed tremendous disgust. Frustrated Moo was in the midst of one of the longest losing streaks in the cave's history.

"Kla?" Ton asked.

There was almost no hesitation.

"I'll see your ten and raise you ten," my Dad answered confidently.

My Dad dropped his twenty one-thousand-baht bills into the pot. Although he tried to maintain a poker face, I detected a tiny smirk on his lips. My Dad gave his hand away with the too-quick raise as well.

"Twenty thousand to me, eh? I'm in," my brother said.

Had Nid missed Dad's smirk? Nid counted out twenty one-thousands and tossed the bills into the middle of our circle.

"Brave, boy," Ton taunted. "Maybe too brave staying in?"

"What would you know about bravery?" my Dad asked.

The pot was huge. I stared at about two-hundred thousand baht. Too bad I had such lousy cards. Ton tossed another ten one-thousand-baht notes on the pile.

"I'll call. What do you have, Kla?" Ton demanded to know.

As though attached by a weak spring, Ton's head wobbled back and forth on his white neck while he finger tapped. Uncle Moo hovered and stared at my Dad. My father leaned forward reaching out to show his cards.

"Check this out, guys! Two pairs, kings-high pair. Yeah, Baby!" my Dad said.

My Dad grinned magnificently while cocking his arms ready to collect the gigantic pot. I watched Nid floating up and down. Ton didn't change his facial expression. With hunter-like focus, he stared at the mountain of cash. In disgust my younger brother tossed his cards on the dark, dirty, and damp cave's floor.

"I'm out! Son-of-a-bitch!" my brother said.

"Careful, Nid, you'll get those cards wet," Ton scolded.

"You know that we can't buy any more cards. It's against Thai law. No gambling!" Uncle Moo said.

"Ha-ha-ha," we all laughed.

"Damn lousy cards!" my brother said.

I looked at Ton. His appearance said it all.

"Read 'em and weep, suckers. Three jacks," Ton said.

My Dad slammed his fist downward.

"Oh my God," I blurted out involuntarily.

"Glad I cut out when I did," Uncle Moo said.

"Me, too," I said.

"Three J's, boys. Lovely ain't they?" Ton said.

Ton swept the pile of money in his direction. A triumphant grin covered his horribly pale face. My Dad was furious. Losing that pot to Ton cost him terrible disappointment and a lot of money.

"Whose deal?"

"Kla's."

"You sure?"

"Wait a minute! I think I hear something."

"I felt a disturbance."

"Listen."

"I hear bicycles."

"Listen carefully. I hear footsteps, talking, and bicycles."

"Look! It's the Wild Boars soccer team and their assistant coach. They're passing through the first chamber."

"Shit!"

"Them again?"

"Hurry! Pick up!"

"Grab those cards!"

Everyone rapidly gathered and stashed their cash. Ghosts zipped everywhere.

"Get out of here!"

"Retreat!"

"Fly!"

"Uan, move it!"

There wasn't time. The poker game consumed us to the point where we'd let our guards down. Even the dim ambient light from the cave's entrance slowed our reflexes. Any amount of natural light did that to ghosts.

I saw that many of the boys rode mountain bikes. They pedaled fast, as they approached our chamber. I heard chatter and heavy breathing. The boys were excited. Focus! Focus, Uan!

"Everyone fly away! Now!"

"Go! Go quickly!"

"Ssshhh."

Uncle Moo raised a finger to his white lips, as he flew away. The others followed in a flash. As usual, I lagged behind. I could see that one card still lay on the cave's floor. Go get it or not? Oh, no! I didn't have time to retrieve it. Leave it! Another foolish mistake. As I disappeared into the darkness high up near the cave's ceiling, I watched one of the boys walk over and bend down. He picked up the card. I paused momentarily and listened.

"Hey guys, look what I found!"

The other boys circled the boy holding the card.

"Wow!"

"That could be an omen."

"Cool!"

"An omen of what?"

"What's an omen?"

"Told you this place was haunted."

"Believe what you want."

"How did it get here then?"

"Maybe local gamblers."

"Gambling's illegal in Thailand."

"Ha-ha-ha."

"Don't know."

"Me neither."

"Maybe we shouldn't go in today."

"I've got the willies."

"Me, too."

"We've never had a problem here in the past."

"Have we ever been here in monsoon season before?"

"You okay?"

"Guess so."

"You guys?"

"Yeah, sure. It's probably nothing."

"Don't know."

"Stay alert!"

"Bring your phones for torches. Leave the bicycles there on the railing. Lock 'em up, boys."

"Anyone got any food or water?"

"Very little."

"Not me."

"Me neither."

"Forgot mine."

"Ate my snack already. He-he-he."

"Take whatever you've got."

"Okay, we won't stay too long."

"Yeah, I'll be hungry soon."

"Let's go!"

"Looking forward to Mom's cooking."

"Mmm."

"I'm going to eat spicy tonight."

"Yum."

"All right, everyone?"

I followed along the ceiling's contours, as I retreated deeper into the cave. From Chamber 3, I glanced back to see the boys finish locking their bicycles. I couldn't hear them anymore. Several bikes still had water bottles on them. I guessed that the bottles were empty, or the boys probably would have taken them along. Surely they won't be in the cave too long.

A couple of the boys had seemed like they needed a little convincing to enter the cave, but the others were ready to explore. Brave and adventurous kids. Oh, to be young again. I could only dream. I wished that my life had turned out differently. Move on. I sighed. Nothing you do now is going to change the past. Focus on the future. What's done is done.

To my great surprise none of the boys seemed the least bit concerned about the weather. During a strong Chiang Rai downpour, the cave fills up quickly. Didn't they know that? Over the years we ghosts have found tiny gaps in the karst which only we can pass through. Even when all of the chambers are flooded, we can still do an end to end run of the place, but boys would get trapped. I scratched my head.

I felt pretty confident that the boys wouldn't risk going past Sam Yak—a T-junction over a mile from the cave's outer entrance. By the way, in Thai 'sam' means three and 'yak' intersection, so 'sam yak' is a three-way intersection or a T-junction. The boys couldn't travel through flooded passageways. I survived being trapped in a cave, but they couldn't. Not a chance.

The boys already had gone past the second chamber and could no longer see the cave's entrance from there. They couldn't monitor rainfall levels. Ton caused me to worry about the boys each time that they came around. He seemed to be in one of his evil moods again. Ton is a murderer and a hungry ghost. I flew up to where my companions were hovering in the next chamber.

"What took you so long, Uan?" Uncle Moo asked.

I hesitated.

"You know that he can't fly as fast as the rest of us," my brother said.

"Yeah, that's why his name is Uan," Ton said.

"Ha-ha-ha, Ton," I faked a laugh.

"Isn't it that same group of boys who we see often?" Uncle Moo asked.

"Yes," my brother said.

"You sure it's the Wild Boars and their assistant soccer coach?" my Dad asked.

"Uh-huh. Yes, I'm absolutely positive," I said.

I didn't like the expression on Ton's ever-reddening face. Ton enjoys killing. What was going on in his murderous mind? I could see him plotting something. I prayed for the Wild Boars each time that they visited the cave. I looked at Ton again. We often had convinced him not to kill, but his hunger grew noticeably the longer that he waited between kills.

My group always listened to the conversations of the Wild Boars whenever they entered our cave. I enjoyed learning about the Moo Pa Academy boys. Down here in the underground, they were a breath of fresh air. The boys usually talked about soccer, school, and food. Sometimes their conversations made my mouth water. I assumed that most of the boys weren't dating yet because they rarely spoke about girls.

When visiting our cave, the Wild Boars usually wore their uniforms. They looked good in them. I always felt a big relief when the soccer boys left the cave unharmed. Although they provided me with entertainment, I often wished that they would never come back. The Wild Boars would be much safer that way.

"They must've come here right after practice," my Dad said.

"Ugh, those damn kids are full of life and energy. Imagine that. Play soccer for a few hours and then hike and ride bicycles to go spelunking. Wish *we* had that kind of freedom and weren't stuck here. My fucking boss! All because of his beautiful daughter, the princess.

"Arghhh, while I want to leave this shit hole, these boys want to visit it. Come play in here. What's the thrill of being in this dump? I don't get it. Wish I had their energy level again," Ton said.

"Forget it, Ton. You didn't even have that energy level when you were alive," Uncle Moo said.

"Ha-ha. Good one," my brother laughed.

Ton elevated and began shaking his ugly, white index-finger at Uncle Moo.

"Watch yourself, Moo. Bad things can happen down here. Remember, I've still got the knife," Ton warned.

Ton rubbed his white hands together. Uncle Moo crossed his arms. He wisely kept his mouth shut.

"Let it be," my Dad said.

My father is the oldest in our group, and I for one felt he is the wisest. I'm sure that Ton would have disagreed with me on that point. Ton raced about here and there. Uncle Moo avoided Ton. We all glided a small distance from each other in formation. We flew single file by the time that we'd turned left at Sam Yak. We probably wouldn't have much peace and quiet until the boys left the cave. I hoped that they would be gone in an hour or so.

Moody Ton. In the darkness would he try to stab a boy? I prayed not. His knife. That damned knife. That knife had gotten us stuck here, and maybe someday it would get me out. Ton never let his murder weapon out of his sight though. Only through trickery could one ever hope to wrestle it from him.

I knew that Uncle Moo and my brother Nid would side with Ton if something came down to a vote. There was some bad blood between my father and his younger brother. Somewhere along the line my father had done something to turn my brother Nid against him as well. Dad never wanted to talk about it, but whatever it was, my brother never forgave Dad.

It pained my father that he never could reconcile with his youngest son. Although I tried to help the two mend old wounds, nothing ever came of my efforts. Nid feared Ton and with good reason. Nid may have even respected Ton in some weird way. Uncle Moo felt similarly toward Ton. My father and I would stick together. We always did. My Dad is a good ghost.

Chapter 2

"I hate when these damn kids come in here with their assistant coach acting like they own the place," Ton said.

"Yeah, this is our home," my brother agreed trying to win some brownie points with Ton.

"They don't even know that we live here," Dad said.

"They don't even know that we live here," Ton mimicked in his falsetto voice.

"They don't even know that we frigging live here," Ton repeated while waving his hands in the air like someone trying to stop a buffalo.

"Pff," my Dad said.

My Dad turned his head sideways.

"No, they don't," I added.

"You heard 'em talking, Uan?" Uncle Moo asked.

"What the hell was that all about?" Ton asked.

"Umm, in the hasty scramble we missed a card. They found it, but there's nothing to worry about. That card could've been left by some Thais who were gambling. I'm sure the boys will be gone soon. It's raining," I said.

I tried to assure Ton that the Wild Boars weren't a problem.

"Well, I'm worried. I'm damn worried, and I'm in a bad mood. I've got the cave blues. I've got an urge to kill. Keep an eye on those kids. Be vigilant. We can't have them discovering our sleeping chamber," Ton said.

"Ton, they'll never go that far past Pattaya Beach," my Dad said.

"Probably not. I don't think they'll even go past Sam Yak," I added.

"They won't if they know what's good for them!" Ton said angrily.

"Ton's right though, we need to be on the lookout," my Dad said.

"Yeah, we're vulnerable in the sleeping chamber," Uncle Moo said.

"Oh, I'm sure they never in a million years would go that deep," my Dad said.

"They'd better not! Not during monsoon season!" I said.

"This cave floods," my Dad said.

My Dad's face showed signs of deep concern.

"This cave floods," Ton repeated in a haunting voice while slapping his leg.

"Yes, it does," my Dad said.

"Floods real badly. They could be trapped," I said.

"They could be trapped," Ton repeated in his falsetto.

"They're just boys," my Dad said.

"I hope that they do get trapped. I want more blood! Teach them all a final lesson about going into caves," Ton said.

"We're not going to harm those kids," my Dad said.

"Speak for yourself. I want blood!" Ton said.

"Well it's not going to be theirs," my Dad said.

The white wrinkles on my Dad's forehead looked like rows of red-ant eggs at a market. I hadn't seen him this stressed and upset for years.

"It's not going to be them," I added.

"Then who's it going to be?" Ton asked.

Everyone tensed up. We gave Ton more space. Silence filled the chamber.

Please. Please, boys, exit the cave. With flooding already underway, I suspected that a big rainfall would quickly trap them. Who knew what bloodthirsty Ton would do if the boys became trapped? He'd been needing a kill for a long time. If any boy became separated near Ton … I couldn't complete that thought.

For years we'd been convincing Ton to sacrifice only snakes and small mammals that lived in the cave, but he is a murderer. He wanted and actually seemed to need human blood. Ever since that fateful day. If given the chance, Ton would kill again. What additional consequences would he suffer? He already lived in the underground. I prayed that no boy become isolated. Uncle Moo and Nid wouldn't try to stop Ton.

I didn't believe in killing and neither did my Dad. Witnessing one murder was more than enough for me. Ugh, I felt sick to my stomach even thinking about the past. These boys seemed so innocent. Perhaps that drove Ton's hunger. I couldn't let anything happen to the Wild Boars. My Dad felt protective of the boys too.

As the years went by in Tham Luang Cave, we evolved a democratic system with each of the five of us possessing one vote. We employed that system to resolve difficult issues when there was disagreement in the group and no compromise could be reached. As far back as I could remember, my uncle and brother never voted against Ton. The three of them formed an unbeatable alliance.

Perhaps Uncle Moo and Nid always sided with Ton because they feared that he would retaliate if they opposed him. It was their basic survival instincts. Surely Ton didn't have enough money to buy them off each time. Did he? In the underground we played a zero-sum game with our money. We couldn't afford graft payments as easily as they could above ground.

Ton is a bad seed. He is extremely dangerous; his anger burns. We all had seen him kill an innocent man. Ton thrives on killing. No one of us could combat Ton alone. Dad and I would have our hands full if the Wild Boars and their assistant coach became trapped.

"Those kids are coming deeper," my brother said.

Nid's white hand cupped his ear.

"Unbelievable," Uncle Moo said.

"Eh?" Ton said.

"They're still coming," my brother said.

"Let's head for Pattaya Beach," Uncle Moo said.

"I'm with you, Moo," my brother said.

"Yes, retreat is an excellent idea," my Dad said.

"We need a plan," I said.

And, just like that, the five of us were retreating in our own home. We all enjoyed the oxygen-rich air between the second and third chambers and liked to play cards there. I suppose that it was the closest any of us would ever come to freedom. While the boys remained in the cave, we wouldn't be able to hang out at our favorite spot. I trailed slightly behind the others, as we went farther underground.

"… making plans, let's wait for Uan," my Dad said.

I heard my Dad finish his sentence just as I was catching up to the group at the Pattaya Beach air pocket. Had he begun "Before we start"?

"Hey, slow poke. Glad you finally made it," Ton said.

Uncle Moo and Nid nodded, and zipped back and forth demonstrating their own exceptional speed.

"Did you get stuck in one of the tight passages?" Ton said.

"Ha-ha," Uncle Moo and my brother laughed.

"Oh, come on," my father said. "Give Uan a break. We only just arrived here ourselves."

"Give Uan a break," Ton mimicked.

I looked at my Dad and then at Ton. These two ghosts were opposites in every way. Sometimes I wondered if Ton didn't act the way that he did simply to impress or oppose someone else. Unlike a typical Thai person, it was in Ton's nature to be confrontational. He thrived on conflict.

During our time together in the underground, I'd gotten to know Ton far better than I ever had wanted to. I didn't like my cousin. That dislike was transforming quickly into a true hatred. I wouldn't be able to tolerate him much longer. What could I do? No solution ever had presented itself.

I reflected back to a lesson that I'd learned in the world above ground: do unto others as you would have others do unto you. Not following that principle there had been a big mistake and landed me in the cave. I promised myself that I would stand in the way of Ton if he threatened the Wild Boars or their assistant coach. Deep down inside though, I knew that it would be horribly difficult to win a war against Ton.

Within a mile or so after departing from Sam Yak, we were powwowing about what to do about the soccer team. Fuck me! Why did I have to end up in the same cave as Ton? He was probably the meanest ghost in all of Chiang Rai, perhaps even the northern part of Thailand. My Dad and I needed to play our hands right, or several of the Wild Boars might never be heard from again. That thought troubled me immensely.

"You know it pisses me off to no end that these kids come waltzing into our home whenever they feel like it. They leave footprints. Throw trash everywhere," Ton said.

"They're Thais," I said.

"Oh, Ton. Give 'em a break," my Dad added.

"We throw stuff on the ground too," I said.

"Like what, smarty pants?" Ton asked.

"Toilet paper. Plastic bags. That card," I said.

"Damn that card! Those kids may start exploring farther in here due to that fucking card! I might just have a surprise for them if they come in here," Ton said.

"And what might that be?" my Dad asked.

"You'll see when the time comes," Ton said.

"The time comes?" I asked.

"Yeah, when the time comes, asshole!" Ton said.

Ton gripped the back of his own neck and squeezed hard. His head glowed.

"Oh, okay. Excuse me," I said.

I wanted to add 'Mister Big,' but I feared that Ton would retaliate in some way against my Dad or me, or perhaps even worse, against the Wild Boars or their assistant coach. No need to agitate Ton even further. My Dad and I glanced at each other. I could see that my Dad felt as nervous as I did about what was transpiring, where things seemed to be heading. The Wild Boars would be in trouble if they didn't leave the cave soon. Be smart, boys. Please think.

"Let's stay together. Let's be a team," my Dad said.

"Let's be a team," Ton sarcastically mimicked my Dad's voice.

Nid and Uncle Moo snickered. They laughed with Ton. My Dad and I hovered closely together. Etched on my Dad's white face, I could see great trepidation. During the one mile of flying deeper into the cave, I'd made some mental notes about the terrain. I thought about the amount of time that it would take the Wild Boars to penetrate to this point. If it poured like hell, I could guess where they might get trapped. I prayed that the rain would let up.

I hoped that the Wild Boars wouldn't go in anywhere near as far as Pattaya Beach. I knew that the boys would be in extreme danger if they did. Ton, on the other hand, would be delighted. The boys would be sitting ducks for him once that far into the cave.

I figured that Ton would pick them off one by one like grasshoppers being removed from corn plants. In that scenario no one from outside of the cave would ever even know the truth about how the boys died. Ton would be a hero of the underground. We all would be heroes. I didn't want to be that kind of hero.

If I could just leave a note inside a plastic bag attached to the cave's wall where the boys could find it, I could provide them with a warning to get out of the Tham Luang Cave as soon as possible. Would they even be able to read such a note? Was it too late already? With their phone batteries weakening, I would need to get a note to them soon.

Leaving such a note would violate ghost protocol. Screw ghost protocol, but I couldn't. I knew that if Ton, Nid, or Uncle Moo found out about such a note, there would be hell for me and my Dad to pay, and the Wild Boars too. Ton would be extremely disturbed, and I didn't want my Dad to go through more hell than necessary. Ton would demand additional human sacrifices in a state of heightened agitation. I wouldn't be allowed to fly for a year. My Dad probably would be grounded too. We might even drown if we couldn't fly. I couldn't do that to my Dad.

Drowning is a horrible way to die. For a ghost once your lungs fill with water, you dissolve from the inside out. You vomit almost endlessly regurgitating parts of your inner organs. The melting of your insides and breakdown of vital tissues is a slow process. The death is excruciatingly painful. Your remains will float in underground rivers filled with the feces of bats and rats forever. And although you've dissolved and disintegrated, the pain sensors in your being continue to exist and feel eternal suffering. At that point there's no chance of any redemption.

The Wild Boars appeared to be traveling exceptionally light. My guess was that the boys would just go to Sam Yak, turn around, exit the cave, and head home.

Chapter 3

Later on the evening of June 23rd after we'd settled into our sleeping chamber, the group wanted me to go back out on a reconnaissance mission to follow up on the boys' activity. Ton, Uncle Moo, and Nid were drinking heavily when I departed. By now, I didn't really expect to see the Wild Boars, unless I caught up to them unlocking their bicycles and riding out of the cave. I assumed that they'd left the cave already. No harm in making sure.

I traveled about 400 yards and reached a dry ledge that we call Diving Board. From the dripping water in the cave, I could tell already that rain poured down heavily outside. I became alarmed. I made my way another quarter mile over to Pattaya Beach. There I could see the water level rising quickly on the cave's floor.

After flying a bit farther, I encountered the Wild Boars and their assistant coach. I felt shocked and disturbed. What were they doing here? This deep? They already went past the area that everyone called Upside-Down Shark's Fin—a steep decline followed immediately by an equally steep and same-length incline. Had the cave already flooded to the point where the boys were unable to retrace their steps to Sam Yak and get out?

Due to the rushing water and my distant stealth position, I couldn't make out the Wild Boars' conversation too clearly. But, when what appeared to be a couple of their scouts returned, here's what I thought that I heard.

"Yikes, the exit is blocked."

"No!"

"Oh, no!"

"Knew that we shouldn't have come in here today."

"Remember the omen?"

"Maybe the cave is haunted with ghosts."

"You guys totally sure that we can't get out by going back?"

"Yes, certain. The cave is flooded. We've been in here too long and went too deep."

"The water level's rising."

"No chance of going back to Sam Yak?"

"None. There's no chance of retreat that way."

"Don't panic."

I thought that I saw a couple of the boys crying. Several of them joined hands.

"You saw no possible way out?"

"That's right. Brown running water is filling up the cave quickly. At Upside-Down Shark's Fin, I ducked my head under, but I couldn't see anything.

There's very little air gap. I couldn't make any progress. The current was pushing me backwards. A drowned rat floated past."

"Another omen?"

"What does omen mean?"

"Yeah, we almost got separated."

"I'm scared."

"Me, too."

"No chance of going back?"

"Not now. I'm worried."

"Same same."

"Oh, boy."

"My parents."

"Stay calm."

"I'm scared."

"You already said that."

"It's so dark."

"What should we do?"

"Don't know. Really confused."

"What about your phone?"

"I dropped it."

"Oh shit."

"What are you thinking?"

"I know this cave like the back of my hand. We're okay. We'll need to go a bit deeper for now, but when the rain lets up, the cave will quickly drain."

My worst fear had come true. The flooded cave blocked the boys' exit. If only they'd turned around sooner, but they hadn't. Now what?

"We left our sandals and bags behind."

"You'll be fine. Your feet are strong."

Thai boys have strong feet, but I worried that one of the boys might get bitten by a snake or scorpion. Without any footwear a slip could happen easily. If someone broke an arm or a leg … Uan, don't think about all of the possible what-ifs. I guessed that they'd left their shoes behind to keep them dry. Another big mistake?

"My Mom will be worried sick."

"My Dad, too."

"My family, too."

"Mine, too."

"All of our families and friends."

"I was expected home."

"Someone will call the coach."

"I know my parents will."

"Mine, too."

"Someone will come looking for us."

"You think?"

"Did you tell anyone where you were going?"

"Not me."

"Me neither."

"Nope."

"My family thought that I was just going to soccer practice and then maybe to buy a snack at Seven."

"Same here."

"That's right, to Seven-Eleven."

"Look, boys, we'll be fine."

"Everyone have faith."

"All we need to do is stick together like a team."

"We're the Wild Boars."

"All for one and one for all, guys."

"Stay together."

"We'll be outta here before you know it."

"Yeah, and this day will become just another memory."

"Anyone got a torch?"

"Just our phones."

"Let's conserve our phones' batteries for now. I'm not sure how long we'll be in here."

"I'll turn off my phone."

"Me, too."

I bumped my head on a stalactite and dropped down about two feet. None of the boys noticed. I hovered in darkness maintaining my distance.

"My battery is getting low."

"Shut it off."

"I feel cold."

"You two, shut off your phones as well."

"Let's leave these other two phones on. Try to save battery life. Reduce the brightness level."

"Shine your phone over here."

"It's so dark."

"I'm sure that we'll get out of here soon."

"Okay, guys. Let's move a bit deeper. I can see the water level rising."

"I'm worried."

"Don't be scared. I'm sure we'll get out of here okay. This rain won't last forever."

"It's monsoon season."

"Will they come looking for us?"

"A rescue team?"

"In Chiang Rai?"

"There are some cavers in the area."

"Not sure, but we need to move now."

"Let's head for Pattaya Beach."

And so went, the troubling conversation of the group of 13. Is 13 an unlucky number? Oh, forget it. Now the Wild Boars were heading deeper into the cave. Even in the darkness, I could see terrible fear etched on their faces, and I could hear the cracking of their voices.

I guessed that the Wild Boars probably ranged in age from around 12 to 16. Maybe one of them was even younger than that. I figured that the assistant coach, their leader, was in his mid-20s. From what I'd seen, it looked like the assistant coach had been a calming influence.

I scratched my head. The youngest of the boys probably hadn't even hit puberty yet. Shit, his family is going to be worried as hell if he doesn't make it home tonight. All of the families will be incredibly worried. What am I going to do? I decided to retreat farther into the cave just ahead of the boys. Maybe there was some way that I could help them.

Chapter 4

I guessed that by now Ton, Uncle Moo, and Nid were pretty hammered. They drank themselves silly on most nights, especially when we had company. If I figured out a way to assist the Wild Boars, I needed to make sure that Ton didn't find out about it. He probably wasn't going to fly drunk with all the rivulets in the cave, so I didn't have an immediate problem. Hmmm. How to assist? Think, Uan.

As the boys walked in my direction, I retreated into the cave and flew about ten body lengths ahead of them. I stayed out of sight yet I wanted to remain within earshot. What they said might give me a clue as to how to help them out. Have courage, Wild Boars, and don't give up. You must have courage, boys.

"My feet are all wet."

"Mine, too."

"Yeah, we're going to have wet and soggy feet until we get out of here."

"Maybe I should have kept my sandals on."

"You can pick them up on the way out."

"I screwed up one of my toenails when I hit it on a rock. I felt it, and I cracked it badly. I think I'm bleeding."

"Hang in there. You won't die."

"My shirt is all wet."

"Mine, too."

"We're all wet. Soaked."

"How will we know when the rain stops?"

"You'll see that the cave isn't filling up as fast, and the water isn't running as quickly."

"That, and the dripping from cracks and the ceiling will slow."

"Is this bat shit?"

"I'm thirsty."

"Same here."

"We all are."

"There's not much to eat or drink. We're going to need to conserve our resources."

"Are we going to get out of here tonight?"

"It's hard to say right now."

I could have told them there was no way in hell that they were getting out of Tham Luang Cave tonight. What would the point of that be though? Such a statement only would decrease their hope and increase their worry. When would they be able to escape?

"If we need to keep going down and the rain continues to fall, we may have to spend the night."

"Spend the night?"

"No choice."

"Oh!"

"The cave has a constant temperature."

"What about ghosts?"

"Now I'm really worried. I'm scared."

"Me, too."

"What about that omen?"

"Don't worry."

"We have each other. We're a team. We'll stick together and take care of each other. Don't worry, guys, we'll get through this. We'll find a way out."

"We have to right?"

"My parents."

"I promise you that we'll all get out of here safely."

"I just want to go home."

"Me, too."

"We need to deal with reality."

"Be calm inside."

"I trained as a monk. I'll teach you how to remain calm and peaceful."

I listened with sharp ears. With the rain continuing to fall, I knew that the boys would be stuck in the cave for multiple nights. Could they survive a few days down here? The longer that they spent in the cave, the weaker and more desperate they would become. Their cuts would become infected. The dampness would cause an irritating fungus to form on their skin. Ton would grow impatient and demand a kill.

I decided to return to my companions and fill them in on what I'd learned. How could I handle Ton? Would I be able to get some time alone with my Dad to discuss possible strategies for helping to get the Wild Boars out of the cave? How much longer would it rain? Would the entire cave system flood? What were the boys doing two-and-a-half miles into the cave at this time of year?

I asked myself a lot of questions, but I didn't have any satisfactory answers, at least not at the moment. As I began working my way deeper into the cave to reach the others, still no answers came to me. I crossed Pattaya Beach and continued onward. This time the journey was more arduous. After another 400 yards, I passed Diving Board. From there it was another 400 yards to our well-concealed sleeping chamber.

I felt just as confused and helpless about the situation as the Wild Boars were themselves.

Chapter 5

My mind raced uncontrollably as I reached the sleeping chamber. My Dad's face displayed an apprehensive look. The three stooges were still passing the bottle of hard liquor around and taking gigantic swallows. My Dad saw me, but didn't break his silence. Then Ton noticed me, too.

"Uan, well boooyyyy, what dah see? Where doze Boars and what dah dey doin'?" Ton asked.

"Yeah, taalllkkk, fatty, what duh, umm. Oh, yeah, what dah ya see?" my Uncle Moo asked.

"There's no reason for insults," my Dad defended and assumed a standing posture.

"Deer's no reasa fer insets," Ton said in his falsetto.

"He-he-he, I'm druuunnnnk," Uncle Moo said.

"Me, tooooo. I'm shit faaaccceedddd. Da. Da. Duh," my brother said.

"I'm gonna paaasssss ert. Gimme dat bot tell," Ton demanded.

Ton wobbled, but he managed to reach up. Woozy Uncle Moo handed Ton the nearly empty bottle of Maker's Mark. In slow motion Ton took a huge swig. As Ton started to pass the bottle back to Nid, Ton fainted. My brother grabbed the bottle, as it fell from Ton's grasp.

"Whew, I'm gonna paaasssss ert, too. Taken this bot tell, ha-ha-ha," my brother said.

I moved closer and saved the bottle just in the nick of time. Nid's breath reeked horribly of alcohol. Uncle Moo slouched over. I set the bottle down. Although I wanted to take a shot, I refrained. I needed a shot. My will power won out.

When my Dad and I were sure that the three drunkards were soundly asleep, we moved away from them to another part of the chamber. We kept the three within our sight just in case any of them woke up unexpectedly. Unlikely, but with a ghost, it is possible.

"What did you see, Uan?" my Dad asked.

"Dad, it's been raining like hell. The boys are definitely going to get trapped tonight and maybe even for days. The water level is rising steadily and quickly. Areas are flooding fast. Upside-Down Shark's Fin isn't passable. The Wild Boars didn't get out in time.

"We need to do something before Ton does. I'm worried. Really worried. The boys will end up past Pattaya Beach tonight. Maybe go to Diving Board," I said.

"Dammit! Oh, son. That's not the news that I was hoping to hear," my Dad said.

"Sorry, Dad," I said.

"It's not your fault. We've got a very unfortunate and delicate situation on our hands, Uan. Very unfortunate. I sure wish that those boys had turned around at Sam Yak," my Dad said.

"Me, too. But they're in here now. What's the plan? We need a plan," I said.

"If it keeps raining, I'm guessing that the boys are going to settle on the ledge at Diving Board. That's a high, dry point. Ton isn't going to like it," my Dad said.

"That's for sure. He wants a kill," I said.

"Somehow we're going to need to protect the boys," my Dad said.

"Yeah, but how?" I asked.

"Not sure. The Wild Boars are going to make this harder on us, as they get closer to this chamber," my Dad said.

"I'm guessing that they won't go farther than Diving Board. But, then again, I didn't think they'd go past Sam Yak," I said.

"There's really no way for them to get out of here," my Dad said.

"Near Diving Board there is a small trickle of water that they could drink from. I'll need to make sure that they find it. They'll soon be thirsty and out of water. Food, too," I said.

"We can't do much about the food situation," my Dad said.

"How long can they go without food?" I asked.

"If they sit still, maybe five or six days," my Dad said.

"They'll be hungry as hell. What about water?" I asked.

"Maybe a little bit longer," my Dad said.

"Don't worry, I'll lead them to water. Drinking water isn't the main issue," I said.

I flew around in small circles to help me clear my head. My Dad hovered in one spot with both hands under his chin. The other three hadn't budged. My Dad seemed to have come up with an idea.

"I'm going to suggest to Ton that you be the one to spy on the boys and report back about what you see. I'll be the one who stands lookout there," my Dad said.

My Dad pointed to the bend just at the start of our sleeping chamber. From there to Diving Board was around 400 yards.

"Will Ton go for that, Dad?" I asked.

"The other guys are lazy. So, yeah, I think they'll agree to let us do the work. You'll come back and give updates to us.

"Whatever you do, don't let Ton know that we are trying to help the boys get out of here. When an opportunity presents itself, we'll do what we can for them. If you need to tell me something important, just be patient.

"Don't say anything in front of Ton or the others that incriminates us. We'll be breaking ghost protocol," my Dad said.

"Fuck ghost protocol!" I said.

"Ssshhh," my Dad said.

"All right. God, I wished the Wild Boars hadn't come in here during monsoon season," I said.

"Yeah, and it's unfortunate that Ton is in such a bad mood. What were those boys thinking? Their assistant coach? Their parents must be worried sick. Someone is sure to report them missing. We'll be getting more company soon," my Dad said.

"More opportunities for Ton. Think of their parents," I said.

"Son, we need to handle Ton with care. Be watchful of your brother and Uncle Moo. I don't trust them around Ton," my Dad said.

"Ton's mood is only going to get worse without his ability to get any fresh air," I said.

"I think the poker games helped to put him in a better mood. He became more stable," my Dad said.

"Especially when he was winning," I said.

My Dad and I smiled at each other. We tried to maintain our hope that the Wild Boars would be safe. Dad patted me on the shoulder.

"When do you think someone will attempt a rescue, Dad?" I asked.

"I don't know, Uan. Like I said, someone will undoubtedly report the Wild Boars missing—a parent, relative, or friend. They'll call the coach. When the coach can't reach the assistant coach, alarm bells will go off. These boys come from good families. What could a team of rescuers do anyway though? I don't see how they could get to the boys," my Dad said.

"It would take an awful brave bunch to enter a flooded cave with rising waters. Upside-Down Shark's Fin is submerged. Between there and Pattaya Beach another passage is submerged too," I said.

"Great. Just great. The water will have a strong current in those flooded passageways. The water's going to be muddy. Like coffee," my Dad said.

"There are cave divers in Thailand. Remember we heard that rumor about a few divers getting close to a sleeping chamber in one of the caves in the south? Was that in Satun?" I asked.

"I vaguely recall. Don't remember the details. It might have been Perlis, Malaysia. Umm, I think you're right, it was near Satun. Not sure if those were divers or just spelunkers," my Dad said.

"Anyway, maybe cave divers could help the Wild Boars. That would be very dangerous though," I said.

"With zero-visibility water? I don't think so," my Dad said.

"I guess you're probably right," I said.

"It would be extremely dangerous for anyone to enter the cave at this time of year. Let's hope no one else gets trapped," my Dad said.

"We certainly don't want Ton to have even more targets," I said.

"That would be a disaster," my Dad said.

"I can't bear to think of these things. With additional people in the cave, it'll be almost impossible to stop Ton," I said.

"Ton was a violent person above ground. Ton is a violent ghost. When he gets hungry, there's simply no stopping him," my Dad said.

"Dad, I'm afraid for the Wild Boars. I'm afraid for anyone else who enters the cave," I said.

"Be strong. I know that it's hard for a ghost to have faith, especially after what we've been through, but you must try," my Dad said.

"I'm glad that we're still together," I said.

"Me, too. Let's move these guys to the back of the sleeping chamber. We need to get some rest. I'd rather we moved them than they get woken up by the Wild Boars," my Dad said.

My Dad and I smiled.

"Agreed. We want to avoid them being startled or even spotted," I said.

"Uan, you look really tired. You need some rest," my Dad said.

"Sure, Dad. You, too," I said.

And on that note, my Dad and I took the others to the back of the sleeping chamber. They never showed any signs of waking up, and their loud snoring never abated.

Chapter 6

I've written this book in the English language. Guess what? Above ground I never even learned English. None of the ghosts in the Tham Luang Cave ever did. So how did I produce this story? Ever heard of a piece of software called Google Translate™? That's right, I used Google Translate™ to go from old Thai to modern American English. I used a calculator to go from the metric to the imperial system.

The Wild Boars actually speak a new dialect of Thai, not exactly the same one as I spoke when I was above ground. If some of the translations aren't exact, please forgive me. And, when the Wild Boars really got going, it was hard for me to remember every single thing that they said. I really never could tell who said what. It was just one talking right after the other in rapid succession. Kids these days, I guess. I filled in details as needed to complete the tale and attempted not to take any poetic license.

◆ ◆ ◆ ◆ ◆

"My head hurts," Ton said.

"Mine, too," Nid and Uncle Moo said in unison.

Uncle Moo gripped his head and moaned. Ton scratched at his own eyes to remove the morning crud. Nid barely could move. Uncle Moo's face was contorted from his headache. Nid rubbed his pale forehead. The three were a sorry sight.

"Uan, what did you see last night?" Ton asked.

"It looks like the soccer team is trapped. They probably needed to spend the night in the cave," I said.

"They spent the night?" Uncle Moo asked.

"In our cave?" Ton asked.

"Probably, yes," I said.

"Where?" Uncle Moo asked.

"I'm guessing near Diving Board," I said.

"They're that close?" Ton asked.

"I'm sure they had to go past Pattaya Beach with the heavy flooding," I said.

"We're going to have a sacrifice soon then," Ton said with great conviction.

I was hovering next to my Dad.

"Ton, I suggest that Uan serve as our scout. He can make trips out to see where the boys are and report back to us. He'll track their movements and watch to see if a rescue mission gets underway," my Dad said.

"I'll agree to that," Ton said. "But don't try to help those boys out."

"Yeah," my brother said. "Nothing sneaky, Uan."

"Look, Ton. Only one of us should be going back and forth or we'll risk being discovered by the boys. Or their eventual rescuers if it comes to that. Uan is a good spy," my Dad said.

"Just don't try anything stupid, fat boy," Ton said.

Ton made me feel very uneasy.

"I'll serve as a lookout. I can keep everyone informed if someone is approaching the sleeping chamber. We can then defend ourselves or retreat as appropriate," my Dad said.

"Take cover?" Nid asked. "In our own home?"

"This is our fucking cave! They're in our cave! This ain't no public cave! Don't forget that! These boys are trespassing on our private property! Dammit! Wild Boars!" Ton said.

"We don't want to be discovered," I said.

"Let's not forget whose cave this is, okay?" Ton said.

"Sure, I concur" my Dad said.

"Agreed," I reinforced Dad's statement to appease Ton.

"I need a drink of water," my brother said. "My head is throbbing."

"I need some more Maker's Mark," Ton said.

"Good idea," Uncle Moo added.

Nid flew over and sipped from a wall drip. Then the three resumed drinking from another bottle. Lazy bums.

"I'll fly back up near where the boys are. I'll check out what they're doing and report back to you, Ton," I said.

"Okay, Uan. Go do your thing. Don't get spotted. Don't lead them back here," Ton said.

"I'll take a position over there," my Dad said while pointing. "If I notice anything, I'll signal you guys. Then we'll all need to retreat quietly and quickly."

"Dad, one finger raised will mean I'm alone. Two fingers up will mean you need to retreat to the back of the sleeping chamber. In that case I'll be following right behind you," I said.

"Okay, Uan," my Dad said.

"That sounds good," my brother said.

"Today we'll be confined here," Ton said. "Confined in our own fucking home! Makes me sick!"

"It probably won't be for but a day or two," my Dad said.

"A day or two! It better not be! These damn kids better be out today! After that, I hope they never come back," Ton said.

"I'm sure that they want out of here as much as we want them out of here," my Dad said.

"The longer this drags on the more problems we face. We don't want a lot of people or the media snooping around the cave," Ton said.

"Media?" Uncle Moo asked.

"Yeah, reporter types. We don't want this cave to make the news. We certainly don't want any kind of international incident. You know what that could do to our cave? Our very existence?" Ton said.

"No, not really," Uncle Moo said.

"Dumbass!" Ton scolded.

I watched Uncle Moo cringe.

"Trust me. If this story ever got out on the Internet, the damn thing could go viral," Ton said.

"Uan, you'll need to be very careful when you're spying on the boys," my brother said.

"When you pass by the boys and work your way up through the cracks to the cave's entrance, avoid detection. The longer those boys are trapped, the more likely they'll be bringing in a monk to try and get rid of us," my Dad said.

"Not a monk!" Uncle Moo said.

"If they bring in the Orange, we might all die," Ton said.

"Shit!" my brother said.

"Who said anything about monks?" Uncle Moo said.

"Look, you know how they use monks to get rid of ghosts. Some monks have powerful spells. If cast from a short distance, we would be in big trouble. Real big trouble," my Dad said.

"Don't ever let a monk touch you," Ton said.

"If a monk touches you, you're a goner," my brother said.

"Let's hope that they don't bring any of those monks down here from Myanmar. Those Orange are the worst," my Dad said.

"Look, many monks will just ask us to leave the boys alone. They will ask us to be kind," I said.

"Be kind. What the hell are you babbling on about? Our existence could be in danger, you idiot!" Ton said.

"Uan, stay away from any Orange," my Dad said.

"Come on, we're getting ahead of ourselves," I said.

My Dad moved into his sentry position while the others passed the bottle.

"Uan, go now. Let us know what's happening up there," Ton said.

And with that directive, I flew away leaving my fellow ghosts in their sleeping chamber. I planned to see what the boys were doing, listen in if they were awake, and then sneak past them to the mouth of the cave. I would check them again on my return. The rising waters would make my passage a dangerous one. I prayed that no monks had arrived yet. I feared the Orange more than anything else. What if they had brought some monks in from Myanmar? Concentrate, Uan.

Chapter 7

On my flight back to the Wild Boars, I felt dehydrated. I noticed a nice clear trickle of water coming down near Diving Board. I took a sip. The water refreshed me, and I immediately felt better. I splashed some cool water on my face and instantly became more alert. I blinked repeatedly. I shook my head from side to side. That's better.

The earth above the cave's ceiling filtered the rain water. We were almost half a mile underneath the surface here. The rivulets that had formed on the floor of the cave were muddy and undrinkable. If the boys passed Pattaya Beach and made it to Diving Board, I would find a way to make them aware of the potable trickle.

When I reached the boys, they were huddled together sleeping on the cave's floor. I saw a tangled mass of bodies. Poor kids. A pit welled up in my stomach. The Wild Boars looked all soggy, and so tiny there on the unwelcoming cave's floor. So helpless. I saw no movement. The stress and danger of their situation and lack of provisions probably sapped them of their energy to the point of collapse. As a group, they may have comforted one another enough to sleep.

I stared at the entanglement of humanity below me. Why did I now feel such a great concern for humans? I could see their fragility, their flaws and weaknesses. Why did my Dad and I have to be with Ton on that fateful day? I suppose it was peer pressure, lack of education, and naïveté. Maybe I could redeem myself by helping out the Wild Boars. But how?

"Uan," I whispered to myself.

Hearing my own name helped me to snap out of my reflection. You can be a good ghost. You don't need to follow ghost protocol to the tee. Uan, there's an opportunity here. Like your father, you're a good ghost. I tried to convince myself of that fact.

"Uan," I said again.

I only wished that I'd listened more carefully to my teachers and true friends while I'd been above ground. Look at where bad timing had led me. Now I needed to do a job. I decided to let the sleeping Wild Boars lie and work my way toward the mouth of the cave. As I traveled past the boys, I saw their handprints on the cave's wall. Shoeless, they'd steadied themselves while slipping like hell going up and down the inclines. I marveled at their courage and ability to move in these dark halls. I continued slowly.

Laawt Yaow consists of a series of tiny cracks and tubes that a ghost can use to penetrate through the middle of Upside-Down Shark's Fin. By the way, 'laawt' means straw and 'yaow' means long. Each year we reverted to the long-straw passage once Upside-Down Shark's Fin flooded. I entered Laawt Yaow as a vapor of white smoke and squeezed through. Even a ghost can get stuck in a tiny crack, you know. Especially a fat one.

I needed to be careful. Drowning was a real possibility. I laughed as I wiggled my form through a ridiculously tight spot. Laughing in the face of grave danger. Ha-ha. I shook my vapored head from side to side touching it on the walls. This brushing up against the walls tickled me. I laughed some more.

Since even I couldn't travel in the completely flooded passages of the cave, it took me much longer than usual to traverse the cave. I emerged from a cave wall about halfway between the tip of Upside-Down Shark's Fin and Sam Yak. I pressed on toward Sam Yak. The ground was wet and muddy. I flew when space permitted. I moved carefully and paid close attention to everything.

As I made my way up a steep wet incline, I saw the boys' footprints and some long barefoot slides. Those kids have amazing balance. Another hundred yards farther along I encountered a pile of sandals and bags. I shook my head. I guessed they'd ditched their footwear and gear to keep it dry. If they knew that the cave was flooding, why did they go deeper? Strange. Boys will be boys.

At Sam Yak I turned right. Another few hundred yards of flying. I flew over the boys' bicycles. Suddenly, three Thai soldiers came into view. Shit! Be careful, Uan. I hid myself up near the cave's ceiling. I trembled. Oh, my God, a rescue mission seemed to be underway already.

"Whew!"

Had I said "whew" out loud? None of the soldiers had looked up. So, if I'd said 'whew' out loud, I said it quietly enough. Careful, Uan. The three men who I observed were carrying large steel-cylinder scuba tanks on their backs. Were they steel 80s?

The lead guy was wearing a yellow shirt and wore a baseball cap. They all wore long-sleeve shirts, pants, and shoes. The soldiers must have been very strong, as they walked with ease over uneven terrain despite the heavy cylinders on their shoulders. But what were they doing with those tanks of compressed air?

I hovered quietly and watched the men working. They seemed to be staging the tanks. I surmised that when the Wild Boars' parents reported them missing to the coach, a rescue effort had begun when the coach was unable to contact his assistant coach. Fortunately, the boys unknowingly had left a trail of breadcrumbs for the soldiers to follow.

If the rescuers kept pressing farther into the cave, they would find footprints going left at Sam Yak, a pile of sandals and backpacks, more footprints and slide marks, handprints on the cave walls beyond Upside-Down Shark's Fin, and more foot- and handprints thereafter. But, could the rescuers even get that far? They would need to dive to go past Upside-Down Shark's Fin. A couple of other flooded passageways would require scuba gear as well. Could they follow the breadcrumbs? It would be so dangerous.

Upon finding the mountain bikes and having no evidence supporting that the boys were still above ground, the rescuers surely would have concluded that the soccer team went into the cave and became trapped. Now it appeared as if a full-scale rescue mission was underway. I couldn't begin to fathom the type of complexity that such a mission would require. Ton wouldn't be happy when I reported back.

I needed to piece this puzzle together in my own mind before I returned to the group. What would I have done if I were in the position of the rescuers? Hmmm. Let me think. Anyone who took a look in the cave could see that there was no way for a human to penetrate its flooded passages, that is, unless they used scuba gear.

So, the soldiers bringing in the scuba tanks must have been planning to dive through the flooded passages in order to look for the boys.

With the terribly murky water, it would be damn near impossible. Cave divers? Coupled with Ton's murderous intentions, I feared for the lives of the rescuers as well as the boys.

It didn't really matter why the Wild Boars had entered the cave in monsoon season. They were here now. Okay, think, Uan. I figured that the rescue effort would involve calling some of the people who had been in our cave before. We always kept an eye on anyone coming into the cave. And, in years past, spelunkers came in and mapped the passageways of our cave. Rescuers would need those maps in order to ascertain where the boys might be. Thai people are always willing to help one another, so I knew that such maps could be obtained and that the rescue mission would be well supported. Thais are indeed good at helping other Thais.

The rescuers could easily figure out that the boys took few supplies with them. The soldiers knew that the Wild Boars would be needing food and drinks shortly. With more heavy rains probably on the way, I watched the urgency in the actions of the soldiers. They must have known that there were 13 people stranded in the cave and that they needed to be rescued soon.

It was June 24th. I hovered and continued to observe the operations down below. The soldiers seemed well trained and extremely well organized. They moved deliberately with purpose and as a unit. Their movements looked choreographed. A well-defined staging area for the tanks quickly emerged. Other soldiers brought in some lights. I saw long ropes and some types of specialized equipment.

Even though I didn't dare go past the third chamber, I could tell from the rising waters in the cave that the rain continued to fall heavily outside. The monsoons would make it difficult for the soldiers to continue their rescue efforts. When it appeared to me that the soldiers were retreating from the cave, I decided to make my long trip back to where the boys were located.

I headed back to Sam Yak, turned left, flew over the boys' gear, vaporized, made my way through Laawt Yaow, reintegrated, saw the eerie area with many hand- and footprints, and approached the Wild Boars' position.

Chapter 8

When I returned to the Wild Boars later on June 24th, they were sitting upright and talking. I assumed a stealth position where I could hear their conversation and observe them. The boys turned on one phone for light, but I felt certain that soon they would be in total darkness. What then? I worried for them. I listened to the boys.

"What are we going to do?"

"What can we do?"

"We need to stick together. No one can go off on his own. No one can get separated."

"Yeah, we already have enough problems."

"How long were we sleeping?"

"Don't know."

"A few of us should go in the direction of the cave's entrance and see if that looks any better. If we can exit there."

"I think it rained more last night."

"I hear the water running faster."

"We can't retreat. The triangle passageway will be totally flooded by now."

By 'triangle passageway' I thought that the boy referred to Upside-Down Shark's Fin.

"If we couldn't get through before, we can't get through now."

"We'll be without any lights in another day."

"No way to keep track of time when the phones all die."

As I'd suspected, none of the boys wore a traditional watch.

"Please don't say the word 'die'."

"Sorry."

"You think we'll need to spend another night in here?"

"Don't know."

"If we're going to go deeper to search for an exit, we'd better do that before the batteries in the remaining phones run out."

"What time is it?"

"Four p.m."

"When our last phone dies, we'll be in total darkness."

"I'm scared."

"Okay, stop saying that please. You're not helping."

"Give 'im a break."

"Sorry."

"What if we go exploring and the phone's light dies?"

"Dies?"

"How will we get back?"

"Good question."

"Don't panic."

"We need to hold hands and stick together."

"We'll take roll call to make sure everyone's all right."

"If we split up to explore and the phones die, it will be difficult to get back here in total darkness."

"Please. Please stop saying the word die."

"Sorry. It just comes out naturally."

"I'm worried."

"We can't make any sudden decisions or moves."

"Let's think things through."

I almost cried while listening to the boys. They were fucked. Their situation was hopeless. Although some of the boys worried about ghosts, they didn't know that Ton could strike them down at any moment. If the boys split up into groups, they might get separated and lost in the cave. In total darkness it would be difficult to reunite. Once out of voice range, it would be impossible to find each other again. Oh, Wild Boars. Wild Boars! What could I do?

I decided that I would work a little magic to get the boys to go deeper into the cave. There was no chance whatsoever that they could get past Upside-Down Shark's Fin, the other flooded passages, and make their way back to Sam Yak. If I could get the boys past Pattaya Beach to Diving Board, I could lead them to the water. At least if the Wild Boars had drinking water they would have a greater chance of survival. The ledge there was still relatively dry. Perhaps against my better judgment, I decided to make some noise.

"What was that?"

"You hear that?"

"Don't know. Shine the light there."

"Nothing."

"I'm scared."

"Hope it's not a ghost."

"Shut up."

"It's okay."

"Let's follow that sound. Maybe it was a small animal. He may know a way out."

"Good idea."

"Follow that sound."

I successfully had attracted the boys' attention. Now they moved toward me. If I could just get them to move in the direction of Diving Board as a group. I made more noise.

"Hear that?"

"Yup."

"Me, too."

"Follow that sound."

"Okay."

"Hold my hand."

"Watch your step."

"Walk slowly."

"Everyone here?"

"You're hurting my hand."

"Sorry."

I saw one of the boys shining his phone's light on the group and scanning over everyone.

"I counted twelve. Plus me that's thirteen. Stay together, guys."

"Move slowly."

"Hold hands."

"What do you think that noise was?"

"Don't know."

"I hope it isn't a ghost."

"Me, too."

"If it is, he seems to be friendly."

"Ha-ha, I don't think there are friendly ghosts."

I couldn't help but smile. Just a bit more boys. Come on! Follow me. Please, follow me!

"Oh, shit!"

"What happened?"

"I slipped."

"Be careful."

"Move more slowly."

"Take it easy, fellas."

"Watch your step."

"I can't see shit. How can I watch my step?"

"Shine the light here."

"Can't see you."

"Here. Over here. Listen to my voice."

The boys were struggling up a slippery incline.

"Oops."

"My battery's almost dead."

"Keep moving."

"Follow that sound."

"We need to keep moving. Slowly."

"Easy does it. Easy does it, boys."

"Whoa."

The Wild Boars made steady progress behind me. Eventually, after a great effort, I led them to Diving Board. Just beyond there I found the steady trickle of clean water and flew over to it. I made some noise and then flew up toward the ceiling and out of the way. Out of sight.

"Over there."

"I hear the sound of running water."

"Okay, together."

"Here. Over here."

"Feel that steady drip?"

"It's nice and cool."

"I'm going to take a drink."

"Not so fast."

"Don't drink too much; you might get sick."

"Take small sips."

"How does it taste?"

"Oh God, it's so good and clean. Feels good on my lips. My lips were cracking."

"My mouth feels like I've been in the rice fields all day."

"Don't drink too much."

"That's enough."

"Let me have some."

"Me, too."

"Sure."

"Take turns. Don't overdo it."

"Just enough to wet your lips, guys. A few sips. Don't try to quench your thirst."

"Boy, that's good."

"We're so lucky that animal led us here."

"Wonder where he went?"

"Disappeared."

"I don't hear him anymore."

"Sure it wasn't a ghost?"

"Let's not talk about ghosts."

"My parents believe in ghosts."

"So do mine."

"All Thai people do."

"Thank God we were led here."

"Whatever it was probably took a drink and got scared off."

"Yeah, we frightened him."

"He frightened me."

"What do you think it was?"

"Maybe a rat?"

"Don't know."

"We may never know."

"Just be thankful that we found this trickle."

"I hope it keeps running."

"Let's settle down there on that ledge."

"Good idea."

"It's dry. Well, kind of."

"The water seems clean."

"If no one gets sick, we can continue to drink this water."

"From that little ledge we crossed to here, we can hear one another easily. That way no one gets lost while getting a drink."

"Once it's dark, we'll probably have to crawl."

"I don't think we can do much more now."

"We need the water level in the cave to drop."

"It's a waiting game."

"Do you think it's worth exploring a little before my phone dies completely?"

"Maybe, but we'd be taking a huge risk of getting lost."

"Maybe we should just stay together?"

"I like that idea."

As the boys were deciding whether to explore the cave more deeply in search of an exit, I thought that it would be best for me to return to the others. Those four would begin to wonder if I was okay. I certainly didn't want Ton coming out here. I headed back. I only needed to travel about 400 yards.

When I rounded the bend toward the sleeping chamber, my Dad hovered there on watch. I held up one finger to let him know that I was alone. He waved. I flew in toward him and hovered.

"Everything okay?" my Dad asked.

"Yeah, Dad. The Wild Boars spent the night in the cave, as I'd guessed. There's no hope for them exiting soon. They're now near Diving Board. I think that they can hold out there for a while. They'll have water," I said.

"Come here you two," Ton said.

"Good," my Dad whispered.

Ton saw me return. Dad and I flew over to the others. It appeared as if they'd been drinking most of the time while I conducted recon.

"What da yah see, Uan?" Uncle Moo asked.

"The boys spent the night in the cave. Their lights are almost finished. They've moved into the Diving Board area," I said.

"What? Der dat deep?" Uncle Moo asked.

"Divin' Board yer sey?" my brother said.

"Yeah, I saw them on a ledge there. They won't be able to move much from there, though. Once their lights run out, I think they'll be forced to remain in that area. The boys won't be coming nearer to here. They're all very worried about getting separated. Especially the younger ones," I said.

"Dey should be worriiieeeddd," Ton said.

"Yeah," Uncle Moo said.

"It'd be sooooo easssyyy to grab one," Ton said.

"Ton," my Dad said.

"Oh, I saw Thai soldiers near the cave's entrance," I said.

I attempted to distract Ton from his current train of thought.

"Yer saw dat?" Ton asked.

"Oh meee God!" my brother said.

"I saw a handful of Thai soldiers stockpiling steel-cylinder scuba tanks," I said.

"Rescuers?" my Dad asked.

"Sold-hers?" my brother asked.

"Yes, I think so. I watched them for a while, but they seemed to retreat when the water levels rose. It really must have been pouring," I said.

"Monsoon season," my Dad said.

"See dem any Orange?" my brother asked.

"No. No, I didn't. I didn't get past the third chamber," I said.

Everyone exhaled deeply. There was a brief pause in our conversation.

"I needed to use Laawt Yaow. Upside-Down Shark's Fin is completely flooded," I said.

"Good work, Uan," my Dad said.

"Yeah, goo werk eh er, Uan," Uncle Moo added while slurring his speech.

"Sounds like you had a rough day," my Dad said.

"Not much we can do for now," I said.

"Just hang her, eh? Ha-ha-ha. I said 'her,' " my brother laughed wildly.

"And drin. Drink lots of al-kee-hall," Uncle Moo said.

"Tomorrow you can go back and check on the kids again," my Dad said.

"I hope no Orange show up," I said.

"Me, too," my Dad said.

"The Wild Boars have put us in great danger," I said.

"Yes, unintentionally," my Dad said.

The other three became even sloppier, as the night continued.

Chapter 9

As I tossed and turned during the night, I could hear loud snoring in our chamber. Everyone but me seemed to be sleeping well. June 25th finally arrived. Our group all usually woke up around the same time. When I first looked around, I saw that my Dad's bed was empty. Taking extreme caution, he already had moved to his sentry position. I grabbed a bite. The others were doing the same.

"Uan, you should be off now," Ton said.

"Okay, give me a minute, and then I'll go check things out," I said.

"Do that," Ton said.

"See if the Wild Boars have moved," Uncle Moo said.

"And if anyone else has shown up," my brother added.

"Be careful, son! Be vigilant!" my Dad called over.

"Don't take any unnecessary risks," Uncle Moo said.

"If you see Orange, just back up and return here," Ton said.

"Don't let them follow you," Uncle Moo said worriedly.

"The Orange can't get in here either right now. With all the flooding. Don't worry about me. I'll be fine," I said.

But would I be? I felt worried. Did it show? My fear must have been etched on my face. Was that why I'd received so many warnings from my companions? My fear caused fear in the others. My Dad even came back over closer for the moment.

"I'm starting to feel cooped up," Ton said.

"Hopefully, the boys will get out of here today," my Dad said wishfully.

"Unlikely," Ton said.

Nid and Uncle Moo remained pretty quiet. They both looked badly hungover again. The tension mounted in our chamber. After a few more preparations, I felt ready.

"Here I go," I said.

"Good luck, Uan," my Dad said.

And with that, I flew out in the direction of Diving Board. I made the trip successfully without any real issues. When I encountered the boys, most of them were huddled on the dry ledge. Two boys stood over near the water trickle getting a drink. I felt encouraged to see that they employed the buddy system. If any one of the Wild Boars became separated, he would be in grave danger. Not just because he might get permanently lost, but because of Ton.

Since I saw so little activity, I continued on straight away. I made my way to Pattaya Beach, through Laawt Yaow, past the boys' gear, turned right at Sam Yak, and slowed as I approached the third chamber. I could hear a lot of jabbering. I flew slowly along hugging the ceiling. Watchful.

My situational awareness increased. A few drops of water fell on my back. My heart pounded. I breathed rapidly. Stay calm, Uan. Stay focused. I encouraged myself. Slow your breathing. Inhale. Exhale. I watched for Orange. Thankfully, I didn't see any. Everything else that I saw, though, amazed me.

In addition to the soldiers, I saw a woman and a bunch of other men. I moved into a stealth position from where I could retreat and disappear easily. From my hover spot I could hear most of the conversations down below. I soon learned that the guy in the white shirt with his hands in his pockets was none other than the governor of Chiang Rai. I listened carefully and here is what I heard from those engaged with the governor:

"We must keep looking. We must have hope."

"It's pretty clear based on the video we found on the mobile that the boys are in here."

"Plus their fingerprints on the inner-cave walls, footprints, their locked bicycles. All the forensic evidence indicates they're in the cave."

"Yeah, they wouldn't stay away from home and leave their bicycles here if they weren't trapped."

"No sign of them above ground. Surely there would be, if they weren't caught in the cave."

"We found sandals and backpacks after Sam Yak."

"What's Sam Yak?"

"That's a T-junction. Some people call it Monk's Junction. Left leads to Pattaya Beach—a big air pocket. Right goes a mile or so until it peters out."

"They would have taken their sandals and bags with them if they were able to exit the cave."

"Maybe they're near Pattaya Beach."

"These are good boys. Healthy boys from respectable families. They all attend Moo Pa Academy."

"They're definitely still in the cave."

The governor was convinced that the boys were still in the cave, and he encouraged the search to continue. Thank God for his conclusion. Encouraged by the governor's remarks and his leadership, the group would continue looking for the Wild Boars inside the cave. I wanted to shout 'Hooray.' I watched and listened.

Soldiers brought more provisions into the cave. I couldn't tell who the good-looking doll in the purple blouse was, but she sure was a welcome sight. I hadn't laid eyes on a beautiful woman in years. Had I seen her face before? She looked somehow familiar. No, I guess that I couldn't have.

It surprised me that no one else seemed to take any notice of the natural beauty. They all went right by her. Was she a parent? A nurse? Probably not a nurse, at least not dressed like that. Nurse or not, she could treat me anytime. Maybe she was a volunteer. I honestly didn't have a clue. I just admired her appearance.

As the lovely woman walked in the direction of the cave's entrance, I followed her. I saw a large number of other folks between Chamber 2 and the cave's entrance. Many folks milled around Chamber 1. Were they family members and relatives holding a vigil? What I saw next seriously worried me.

It looked as if a few makeshift shrines had been erected already. If the boys weren't found soon, this foreshadowed Orange arriving on the scene. That would pose a big danger to all of us ghosts. Ton wouldn't be happy. I wouldn't mention the shrines to him or the others. I stayed on high alert scanning the area carefully.

The worried chatter continued below. Thank God that no one ever seemed to look up. They focused on the immediate task at hand. I listened.

"We need to get them out."

"Yeah, but how?"

"Let's keep staging supplies. When the rainfall lets up, we can penetrate into the cave farther."

"We're going to bring in some pumps to try and lower the water level in the cave."

"That's going to be extremely difficult."

"True, but we need to pursue all possible rescue options. This is going to be a highly complex operation."

"Time is of the essence."

"Definitely."

"I'm so glad that you SEALs are here."

"It's our duty."

"Glad that we can help, sir."

"I just feel much better with you guys around. It gives me great hope that we'll get the boys out."

"Don't worry. We will."

"As soon as this rain subsides, we'll be able to get to them."

"I promise we'll get them out."

The training and experience of the Thai Navy SEALs was obvious. They were all well-built, strong, and confident. They were on a mission to get the boys out. It was clear to me that they would either succeed or die trying. Failure wasn't an option. I would aid them as I could. Although I wasn't sure how, I would try. I marveled at the SEALs' courage and bravery. I wished that I was like them.

In a strange way this rescue effort had restored my faith in humanity. I watched and admired as people from different backgrounds worked together. Most looked like volunteers. They came here to help total strangers in need. They made sacrifices to come here. They left their daily lives and families behind to assist in a dangerous rescue of the Wild Boars—boys who they didn't even know. The intense focus of the rescue team moved me. That's right. It moved me, a ghost. I shed a tear and shook. I wiped the back of my hand over my cheeks.

Relatives and friends seemed to be amassing. I knew that the rescuers would soon be going deeper into the flooded cave. They needed cave divers to push all the way to Pattaya Beach. I'd watched enough of the rescue operations for now. I thought about returning to observe the Wild Boars.

I searched for the woman in the purple blouse. Where had the lovely lady gone? She couldn't have just disappeared. After a prolonged search, I gave up. She'd vanished. Having failed in my search, I worked my way back through the ever-more treacherous passageways of the cave. Laawt Yaow, in particular, tested me, and I struggled. As the water level continued to rise, I traveled more slowly and experienced greater difficulty in returning.

Chapter 10

When I reached Diving Board, I saw the Wild
Boars huddled and settled there on the ledge. Quiet
for the most part, I guessed that they were trying to
conserve any remaining energy. The group seemed
to be listening to the assistant coach. It appeared as
though he were training them to remain calm.

The assistant coach had studied as a monk before, as was customary of most Thai men his age,
and was sharing his training with the boys. Good
idea. If he could calm their minds, the Wild Boars
would have a much-better chance of survival.
Without food they would need to remain calm, essentially motionless, or they might starve to death
within the week. Their energy would gradually
wane.

The boys were helpless. I wondered what must
have been going through their minds. I'm sure that
they felt fear and missed their families. Their hunger and craving to eat something spicy, such as pad
ga prao gai, must have been overwhelming. Uncer-

tainty. The black unknown. The self-reproach and feelings of guilt. Poor boys. Hang in there.

Given their predicament, the Wild Boars needed to demonstrate strength beyond their years. Enveloped in darkness, they couldn't help themselves. They were in a prison—confined and only able to battle their own mental demons in isolation. The group formed a small squad. Any larger and they might not have fit in this space; any smaller and the support needed to sustain the group might not have been there.

I didn't notice any casualties yet. Good sign. It would only be a matter of time, though, before Ton would want to come out to Diving Board and see the situation for himself. I worried that if Ton did that, he would single out and murder one of the weaker boys. What would I do then? What could I do? Okay, Uan. Move on. Head back to the sleeping chamber. And with that command to myself, I made the final push back to my companions.

As I approached my Dad's sentry position, I held up one finger. My Dad nodded. I reached him. He looked tired from being on guard duty all day.

"What's up?" my Dad asked.

"More rescuers have arrived. Even the Governor of Chiang Rai is here," I said.

My Dad and I flew over toward the others. We hovered there. I felt so tired that I landed.

"Dat dees yah see, Uan?" Ton asked.

"Yeah, Uan. Waz goin' on der?" my brother asked.

"The Wild Boars are simply resting at Diving Board. They're inactive. Basically just sitting around. Their lights probably are finished by now. Very little they can do, unless the water levels in the cave drop," I said.

"So they'll perish where they are?" my Dad asked.

"Wouldn't dat be niiiccceeee," Ton said.

"I'm not sure, Dad. That's hard to say just yet," I said.

"Did you go up near the entrance?" my Dad asked.

"Yes, I did. Looks like a rescue-operations base is getting set up in the third chamber. The rescue effort is growing. I saw about a dozen people there, including a few Thai Navy SEALs. Many more people in the vicinity of the cave's entrance," I said.

"Da Thai SEALs?" Uncle Moo asked.

"Yeah, Thai Navy SEALs," I said.

"They bringing da SEALs in? Musta be plan plannin' to do da dive," my brother said.

"Diveeee? Weeee." Uncle Moo said.

"Yes, scuba dive. To get through the flooded passageways," I said.

My Dad and I continued while the three drunkards were on the verge of passing out.

"It would be a bold rescue if the SEALs try to dive through that rushing, muddy water," my Dad said.

"Very complex and dangerous operation. I hate to see people risking their lives," I said.

"What would they even do if they found the boys?" my Dad asked.

"Good question. Unless the water level drops, the SEALs would have no way to get the boys out. The Wild Boars are soccer players not cave divers," I said.

"Yeah, they're just young kids," my Dad said.

"I guess the SEALs could bring them food and drinks. Maybe blankets and medicine, until they can be taken out of the cave," I said.

"Could they run an air hose in to reach them?" my Dad asked.

"Not sure," I said.

I scratched my head. My Dad did the same.

"Let's not worry about the details of the rescue, that's not our business. We're just speculating," my Dad said.

"I don't think the SEALs can even find them. And, even if they do, the boys probably will be dead by then," I said.

"If that chamber they're in fills up, they'll all drown," my Dad said.

"What a horrible ending," I said.

"Not da happy one, dat's fer sure," Uncle Moo said.

"Ha-ha-ha," Ton laughed.

"I hope this rain stops," I said.

"The longer this rescue goes on, the more people are likely to enter our cave," my Dad said.

"That isn't good," I said.

"Probably only a matter of time before the Orange show up," my Dad said.

"That's not good," I said.

I didn't mention the little shrines that I'd seen in the vicinity of the cave's entrance.

"No, it isn't. We'd all be in big trouble," my Dad said.

Everyone nodded their heads in agreement. I refrained from telling the others about the good-looking Thai woman whom I enjoyed watching. If they learned about her, they would all want to make the passage up to the cave's entrance. Better keep her to myself. I would enjoy sweet dreams tonight.

"Good work, Uan," my Dad said.

"Yah, go workin'. Fine jab, Uan," Uncle Moo said.

Had Uncle Moo tried to say 'job'? I felt like hitting him with my jab.

"Thanks fer takin' on daaaat chore, Uan," Ton said.

"You're actual look-en a bit thinna already. Ha-ha-ha. All dis here flyin' 'round mey be doin' good fer yah," my brother said.

My once bulging stomach slimmed down. I managed a smile. I hoped that our supply of Maker's Mark lasted until the rescue mission concluded. Once drunk, Ton, Uncle Moo, and my brother seemed to mellow. They became aloof to the Wild Boars' predicament.

Chapter 11

On June 26th I made my rounds again. The boys sat patiently and motionless on their ledge. Did they have any choice? Their strength diminished rapidly. With almost nothing to eat, I'm sure that they suffered terrible hunger pangs. Instead of racing up and down a green-grass field dribbling a soccer ball, all they could do was sit up, huddle for warmth, and try to conserve energy. They looked pathetic.

I saw a group of divers wearing powerful headlamps push farther into the cave, but the strong currents and rising waters forced them to retreat. They made a brave and courageous effort, and excellent progress under dire circumstances. I admired their tenacity.

The number of people between Chamber 3 and the cave's entrance swelled dramatically. The rescue became a major international ordeal. I estimated that there must have been close to 1,000 people in the form of volunteers, government workers, family, military, media, friends, and supporters now in the area. I reported back to my companions with little fanfare, but we were all astounded by the size and scope of the rescue operation. Ton, Uncle Moo, and Nid continued to drink heavily.

♦♦♦♦♦

It occurred to me that the Wild Boars had probably lost all track of time. It was now June 27th, but did they know it? They'd been in the cave now for five days. None of them possessed a watch. By now all of their mobiles' batteries were certainly dead. I wondered how they would survive without Facebook™, YouTube™, updates of the World Cup from Russia, selfies, or gaming. Trapped in the darkness of the cave, they had much-greater worries now though.

The Wild Boars made my daily life a lot more exciting, but too-much excitement wasn't a good thing. The loss of life was a strong possibility. Each day that the boys stayed in the cave, Ton became more restless. It was simply a matter of time before he totally lost it. When that happened, the boys and perhaps even my Dad and I would be in grave danger, especially if we interfered.

The rains hadn't let up; it poured even more heavily, if anything. The water levels in the cave increased, as did the currents in its rivers. Each passing day my recon journey became progressively harder. My waistline shrank. My Dad worried about me. Ton's anger built. I knew that Uncle Moo, Nid, and Ton would leave our sleeping chamber soon. They were all getting antsy and agitated. We all feared the arrival of the Orange.

During my recon on June 27th when I reached Diving Board, several of the Wild Boars were sleeping. The others sat cross legged like young monks. The assistant coach seemed to be keeping them calm. I noticed that the assistant coach wasn't eating any of the meager supplies which the boys had been rationing. From time to time I would see him give his portion of food to one of the younger boys. He bore an enormous responsibility for the boys.

Although the Wild Boars talked little now, what I did hear indicated to me that they hadn't yet given up hope. Where did that hope stem from? The human-survival instinct was indeed a strong one. I gave up hope on them. I didn't want to, but the boys didn't seem to stand any chance of survival. No chance at all.

My greatest hope had become that they died from a peaceful suffocation rather than from a painful Ton-inflicted stab wound. To be about to expire in peace and then be stabbed violently to death would be unthinkably cruel. Only a ghost as evil as Ton could commit such a heinous act.

I knew that the oxygen level in the Wild Boars' chamber had dropped. A horrible stench of feces and urine permeated the air in their room. I couldn't help but admire the courage of the Wild

Boars. They had to grope around with their hands to find anything. All they could do was sit and wait. Just grimly hang on. If even one of them died, I would be greatly saddened. But, it seemed a foregone conclusion. If even one of them survived, it would be a miracle.

When the suffering of a boy became too much for him to bear, the cruel reality was that he would be too weak even to commit suicide. They had no weapon. The ledge wasn't high enough to jump from. Drowning oneself at this spot would be impossible. They were too tired to move. None of them were strong enough to choke another. Suicide by breath-holding wasn't possible since one would merely pass out and not die. They would be forced to endure.

Would they get to the point where they didn't even have the energy to contemplate an act such as suicide? With a misery as great as they suffered from and being in an ever-deteriorating situation, I only could imagine what thoughts might cross their minds. Starvation would be so cruel. I hoped for their sake that the oxygen in the chamber ran out first.

The water levels seemed to rise steadily. The monsoon rains would fall unabated for at least a few more months. No one could outlast the monsoon rains. The skin on the Wild Boars' bare feet would soon start rotting and become infected. They would suffer from numbness, swelling, and eventually gangrene. Malnutrition and lack of activity doomed them. Some would be bitten by nasty insects, rats, or reptiles. Boys, boys, boys! Why did you have to be so curious?

I sneaked past the boys, made my way over Pattaya Beach, through Laawt Yaow, and emerged at my usual spot about a quarter mile from Sam Yak. A bunch of Thai Navy SEALs wearing headlamps startled me. Brave frogmen beat the odds to get this far into the cave. I took great care to move slowly among the stalactites and avoid being noticed.

A few of the SEALs were standing waist deep in water. The water splashed violently against their legs, and the SEALs fought hard to maintain their balance. I saw some red hoses. Were they trying to run an oxygen line in for the boys? Were those guidelines for other divers? I could only speculate.

As I moved farther in the direction of Sam Yak, another Thai Navy SEAL team appeared to be staging more gear. It looked like they'd positioned some guidelines. Would a diver need to pull himself along a rope to make progress while moving into the current? What if someone lost the line?

I carefully made my way past the groups. I shook my head in amazement at their determination and ability. The strong currents in the Thai-tea colored, rushing water must have stopped them for the moment from pushing any deeper. After passing Sam Yak, I reached the third chamber. What I saw there completely blew my mind. It looked like a rescue-operations command center taking shape. Many more people stood around now than before, far too many for me to try and even count.

A small city emerged and supplies had been stockpiled: piles of tanks, dive gear, guidelines, hosing, and boxes of sundries. Moving toward the crowded Chamber 2, there appeared to be more onlookers—parents, relatives, friends, supporters, volunteers, and so on. I risked pushing all the way to Chamber 1 hoping to catch a glimpse of the beautiful woman in purple. I craned my neck, but unfortunately I didn't see her.

I wanted desperately to see the woman in purple again. I decided to push all the way out to the cave's entrance. Wow! Many hundreds of people gathered at the cave's entrance. I scanned the crowd for her, but she wasn't there. I hung my head. Based on the crowd size, I wondered if the Wild Boars' incident hadn't hit all of the major international news outlets already.

In addition to the Thai language and many dialects of Thai being spoken, I heard many different English accents. I thought that I even heard a few other languages being spoken. Was that Japanese? Chinese? Russian? German? French? Italian? I'm no linguist and I'm merely guessing here, but I know that I heard a lot of different languages being spoken.

Groups of Thai soldiers and men carried and pulled large machines. Others followed behind with coils of hose. Were those pumps? Was the government going to try to drain the cave? If so, how incredibly ambitious. Where would the pumped water go? Would it cause local flooding? Was that drilling equipment? Were they going to try and punch a hole in the mountain where they thought the boys were located? Maybe near Pattaya Beach? Were they using locator beacons? What if they miscalculated and hit our sleeping chamber?

I decided to retreat back into the cave. In order to avoid detection, I needed to travel more slowly. I hugged the dripping ceiling. The rising waters transformed my return passage into a perilous trip. Just getting past Sam Yak pushed me to my limits. I now risked everything to gather information about the rescue mission of the Wild Boars.

Horrible fatigue accumulated in my body. Several times on the way back I needed to pause to rest. With all of this strenuous exercise, my gut disappeared. About two miles in from the cave's entrance, I reached a Thai Navy SEAL team again. Were these the same guys whom I saw earlier? This time they retreated. The men looked tired. I admired them. I passed by the SEALs unnoticed. After a difficult squeeze through Laawt Yaow, I pushed past Pattaya Beach and on toward Diving Board.

Chapter 12

When I reached the boys, the terrible stench in their chamber almost made me puke. They remained curled up. A few of them probably had crawled over to drink some water while I'd been away and conducted my recon, but other than that, I saw no signs that any movement from Diving Board took place.

I observed the pile of bodies. I held my nose. The Wild Boars looked like a bunch of chicken parts at a Thai fresh market. The situation looked grim. Watching young people die slowly of starvation in an inhospitable place and being unable to assist, well, it's fucking troubling. How could I help? I didn't want to have to look at the painful scene.

The Wild Boars huddled to conserve warmth. But, it was more than that. As they were about to expire, they wanted to feel another human being's touch. That touch gave them a sense they weren't totally alone. Someone they knew would be there when they died. Someone who cared about

Raymond Greenlaw   101 them. Someone who was in the same predicament. I'm sure that this knowledge gave them a little bit of comfort and peace of mind. Humans bear their suffering the best when they're able to share it with another. I couldn't share my suffering with anyone. Tears welled up in my eyes.

I hardly could bear the scene any longer. Some of the boys rested their heads on the laps of other boys. I could see the bond and love among them. My vision blurred. I wiped underneath my eyes. Get a grip, Uan. I hadn't even felt this bad when we became trapped here. These boys are innocent. Now they would perish with their friends, but without any family present.

I knew that I still had a heart because this tragic scene broke it. From time to time over the years, I heard the news of explosions or collapses of mines throughout the world. The Sumitomo Besshi Mine landslide in Shikoku, Japan in 1899, the Benxihu Colliery explosion in Liaoning, China in 1942, and the Chasnala Mine disaster in Dhanbad, India in 1975 came immediately to mind. But those miners who became trapped presumably knew the risks. Granted, some individuals were forced to work in the mines, but others were getting paid to take big risks. Although miners being trapped and dying underground was a terrible thing, the misfortune of the Wild Boars somehow seemed worse. More un-fair. I watched these kids every day, and I knew about their suffering and courage firsthand.

When I couldn't bear to witness the trial of the Wild Boars any longer, I flew back toward my Dad's sentry point. My emotions led me to speed recklessly. This whole situation was fucked up. How would it end? Despite throwing caution to the wind, I reached my Dad safely. I held up a single finger, as he came into view. My Dad waved. I flew in fast.

"Son, you look tired. Very tired. Almost distraught," my Dad said.

"I am, Dad. I'm totally exhausted. Totally distraught," I said.

"What happened? You're crying," my Dad said.

"The rescue efforts are ongoing, but their rate of progress is slow. Too much water. Too much rainfall," I said.

"Let's get you back there so you can rest," my Dad said.

My Dad moved me back to the sleeping chamber. As the other three started to question me with their slurred speech, my Dad interrupted them.

"Uan is exhausted. He needs some rest. He has nothing urgent to report. None of the rescuers are a threat to us right now. No Orange on the way. Go back to drinking," my Dad said.

"Okay, kay, kay," Ton said.

"Burrrp."

In my near-fainting state, I listened as my Dad concocted a story to avoid my having to be questioned further. My eyes felt heavy; they closed involuntarily.

◆◆◆◆◆

On the morning of June 28th, I reported to my companions about yesterday's findings. Ton went off on a wild tirade about the boys. Uncle Moo and Nid nodded their heads in agreement at various points during his rant. My Dad and I just looked on horrified. I already concluded that the Wild Boars wouldn't make it. But about us ghosts, it seemed only a matter of time before we encountered Orange.

Although I continued my daily runs and reports on June 28th, 29th, 30th, and July 1st, rescue operations to penetrate more deeply into the cave seem to have either failed or been suspended. I always held out hope of seeing the lady in purple again, but so far I hadn't. The Prime Minister of Thailand came to the cave on June 29th. He offered strong support and encouragement to everyone. It was an important step in the rescue operations, and the Prime Minister's words gave everyone more strength and courage to redouble their efforts.

I marveled as the Chamber 3 command center grew in size. Each day more personnel came into the cave. Each day the situation became more urgent. I figured that by tomorrow all of the boys would die. But, I'd said that to myself almost daily for the last few days. The boys' energy levels had plummeted to record lows. Their own hope eventually ebbed. Once the first Wild Boar succumbed, they would fall like dominoes.

Chapter 13

"Uan. Uan, wake up!" my Dad said as he nudged me.

I heard my Dad's voice and felt his hand rocking my shoulder. I'd slept heavily. My exhaustion showed. It was July 2nd. The Wild Boars had been prisoners in the cave for ten days. My Dad and I worried constantly about them. Ton planned to kill a boy today, and then one each day from now on as long as there were any of them still alive.

In a short period of time, all of the Wild Boars would be dead. Dad and I could no longer reason with Ton or delay him. He is a sick ghost and was an evil, murdering man. I desperately wanted the Wild Boars to go out peacefully through suffocation in the comfort of each other rather than dying one by one alone from Ton's stab wounds.

My Dad and I had lost total control of the situation. As I'd done over the course of the last ten days, I prepared to head in the direction of the boys. Ton flew over to me. He grabbed my arm.

"Wait, Uan! I'm going with you today!" Ton said.

I saw that Ton clutched his knife. I looked at my Dad. My father simply bowed his head. We'd run out of options. A Wild Boar would die shortly. Ton needed blood. He would enact his plan. Ton held the deadly weapon. We couldn't stop him.

"Yeah, you go, too," Uncle Moo said encouraging Ton.

"I should've done this a week ago!" Ton exclaimed.

"Better late than never," my brother added.

"Shut the fuck up," Ton said.

My Dad moved to his sentry position. Uncle Moo and Nid looked on as Ton and I departed. Drunken bums. I rationalized things by telling myself that the boys were dead already. I decided to go along with Ton's plan. The two of us talked as we made our way toward Diving Board.

"Ton, the boys usually crawl over to a small trickle and get a drink. That's how they've managed to stay alive. Let's try to isolate one of them while he's getting water. They're so weak, it'll be an easy kill for you," I said.

I could see Ton's excitement build. He would be fulfilled again soon.

"Good idea. Help me isolate one of them near the water. I don't want to scare the entire bunch. At least not just yet," Ton said.

"They can't see anything. They're delirious. As we approach Diving Board, I'll point out where the water's dripping from. You'll hear the trickle. You can circle around once we have a boy isolated," I said.

"Oh, why did I wait so long?" Ton asked rhetorically.

Ton ran a finger over the blade of his knife. He pumped a fist in the air. We continued ahead and reached Diving Board. The Wild Boars looked like 13 thick rice noodles that had been dumped from a hot pot—intertwined, a uniform color, motionless, and limp. The gaunt boys even had a smelly steam coming off themselves. It was a good thing that they couldn't see themselves. Their lack of light was actually a blessing to me.

"There, Ton, you see them huddled together?" I asked.

"It looks like a pile of dead bodies. Are they dead already?" Ton asked.

"They don't move anymore except to get water," I said.

"Are any of them dead already?" Ton asked again.

"Maybe. Not sure," I said.

"Oh," Ton said.

"Ton, stay down! Ssshhh," I warned.

I saw a flash of light in the murky water. The light brightened. Suddenly a diver wearing a bright headlamp appeared as though coming out of a grave. Murky water dripped off his torso. The encumbered diver struggled to the water's edge. Ton and I hid mesmerized. The diver scanned the chamber by shifting his masked face back and forth. As the chamber illuminated, the boys began moving. They were alive! Awakened by the light and commotion about half of them stood up. Perhaps the others were too weak or delirious to stand.

The diver's headlamp revealed a pathetic scene. The boys looked at one another in horror. They looked at the diver with immense joy. The full-geared diver stepped forward. Once illuminated, the boys looked more helpless to me than ever, but I could see great hope in their eyes. Their movements indicated that they actually hadn't quit.

I prayed that Ton wouldn't try to strike now. To extinguish one of the Wild Boars now in the face of newfound hope would have been an unbearable tragedy to witness. If Ton lunged at a boy, I feared that the heavily clad diver wouldn't be able to intercept him in time. I, too, wouldn't be able to do anything against Ton's knife.

What must have been going through the minds of the Wild Boars? Shock. Hope. Excitement. Just to see another human being again, any human, gave them a tremendous feeling of well-being. They might as well have been on the dark side of the moon until that cave diver appeared. They'd been in total darkness for days. Then a second cave diver appeared—the first cave diver's buddy.

What were the cave divers thinking? I could only imagine: Holy shit! We've found them. They're alive. I can't believe it. What a miracle. How are we going to get them out of here? They look so thin. Poor boys. I hope none of them are dead. We're bringing you home. Do they speak English? Can they understand us? The two men began communicating with the boys.

As the men spoke, I detected a strong British accent. The Wild Boars spoke little English, and in their stunned state I wasn't sure if they could comprehend what was being said. I, too, felt stunned. Ton's enormous frustration built. I listened. (Much chatter in Thai by the enlivened boys could be heard. I've included a translation of some of the talk among themselves mixed in here with the conversation that took place with the cave divers in English.)

"Everyone okay?"

"He's speaking in Anglish."

"Anglish?"

"Answer him."

"What he say?"

"How many of there are you?"

"Thirteen."

"Brilliant!"

"Yes, we alive all. Thank you."

"We're going to help get you out of here. We're so happy to have found you. We've some snacks for you."

"Food?"

The cave diver reached into a pouch and pulled out some items that looked like gels.

"Here take these."

"Thanks."

"Here."

"Thank you."

"You've been in the cave ten days."

"Ten day?"

"Oh."

"He say ten day."

"Whoa!"

"Are we England?"

"Could we have gone that far into the cave?"

"We England?"

The boys seemed deeply confused by the British accents. The Wild Boars apparently thought that they traversed the entire earth's diameter and made it all the way to a connecting cave near London. Despite the boys' confusion, the moment of first contact gushed with happiness and amazement. It was fantastic! I almost shouted out "Hooray! Bravo! Exceptionally well done!" But, Ton and I needed to remain undiscovered. Our situation seemed exactly opposite to that of the boys in so many ways.

The divers assured the boys that they would be safe now. Simply finding the boys had shocked everyone. Minutes later and Ton would have already committed a murder. The conversation among the divers and boys happened in a pure and natural fashion. With everyone being so overwhelmed and stunned, the conversation didn't flow, it erupted. Fireworks! Ka-boom!

It was a chance meeting, totally unexpected at that particular moment. The boys hoped to be rescued, and the divers looked for them. But no one realized that contact would be made at that very instant. Wow! The divers did their best to survey the situation and comfort the boys. Together the cave divers and the Wild Boars defeated the language barrier. Everyone smiled. The boys burst with happiness. A few even jumped and landed on their infected feet without pain.

Given the extremely limited energy of the boys, things settled down quickly. The divers talked. I understood that the divers would retreat, inform the operations command center that they'd located the boys, and then devise a plan to get the boys out. Perhaps a doctor would be sent in to monitor the boys. More food and drinks would be delivered. Medicine and blankets. With the location of the boys discovered and the knowledge that they were alive, a rescue plan could be developed to get the boys out of the cave.

Ton expected a kill. Now he realized that wasn't possible. Ton too seemed to be in a state of shock at the emergence of the cave divers and at the appearance of the boys. We remained quiet.

Gradually we decided to retreat to the sleeping chamber.

I didn't want to leave the marvelous reunion, but we needed to. Ton needed to. We stealthily departed from the chamber and made our way back. I couldn't stop shaking my head. I felt an enormous surge of warmth throughout my being. When we rounded the last bend, I held up one finger. My Dad nodded.

Nid and Uncle Moo came over as quickly as they were capable of moving.

"Dad, you're not going to believe this. At Diving Board two cave divers climbed out of the murk right in front of the boys. The boys stood up to greet them. Cheered. What an incredible reunion!

"The divers just appeared out of the void. Talked to the boys in English. They sounded British. Fully geared with bright headlamps. The boys barely understood what the divers were saying. The Wild Boars thought they had crawled through the cave all the way to England! Bloody England! Amazing!

"The divers gave the boys some gels to eat. The boys were starving and ate like hungry catfish. The expressions on the faces of the Wild Boars were priceless. They were stunned and elated to see other humans again. Some jumped up and down on their swollen feet.

"Probably never seen divers before. Until the first diver spoke, they might have even thought that he was some sort of creature. Imagine what was going through their minds. The cave divers seemed shocked, too. The pathetic state of the illuminated boys must have troubled them. So skinny. But pure joy on both sides!" I said.

"I was shocked," Ton said. "I'm fucking shocked. So close to a kill."

"The boys thought they'd made it all the way to England? Ha-ha-ha," my Dad said.

"Real-in?" my brother asked.

"I guess dat der total deliri-ous," Uncle Moo said.

"Yeah, like you and Nid," Ton said.

I held my laughter.

"Yeah, must be after not eating for ten days," my Dad said.

"Maybe the boys felt as if they'd been moving the entire time. I can't fathom a human sitting without any light for that long. Of course your mind would play tricks on you. Nasty tricks," I said.

"What do you think will happen now?" my Dad asked.

Ton suffered from immense frustration. He put the knife away, at least for the moment.

"The divers will go back and tell the outside world that they've located the boys and that everyone's alive," I said.

"That's going to bring great hope to their families," my Dad said.

"Their joy will be immense!" I said.

"Now that the boys have been found they'll be harder to isolate," Ton said.

"I'm guessing they'll bring in a medical doctor who's a skilled diver to examine the boys," my Dad said.

"Yeah, the boys are so weak," I said.

"They'll probably get someone in there to stay with them," my Dad said.

"How long dat well dat be take?" my brother asked.

"Those guys have to make it out. Then they'll need to make plans. Other divers will have to come in. I guess they could make it back in here tomorrow, if they have other divers who are willing to take the same huge risks," I said.

"From what you've seen already, Uan, the rescue operation has so many resources that I'm sure they'll come back again soon," my Dad said.

"I wonder if they'll be able to set up some sort of communications from inside that chamber to the outside world. Will those boys be able to talk directly to their families?" I asked.

"I don't know about that. If they could, it would give them tremendous hope and a great lift," my Dad said.

"I thought the Wild Boars might all be dead before anyone found them. Imagine the joy and relief their parents will feel when they get word that the boys are alive," I said.

"I hoped they wouldn't be. Dammit! What am I going to do now?" Ton said.

"Patience, Ton," my Dad said.

"Patience, Ton." Ton repeated my Dad's words. "I shouldn't have waited this fucking long! Now I can't do shit!"

I smiled inside, and I'm sure that my Dad did, too. In front of Ton though, we would maintain the party line—the appearance that we weren't happy with the boys being discovered. That would be hard to do, though, as I felt truly overjoyed. I may even have slipped up a bit already. Perhaps my Dad had, also. My hope that some of the boys would get out alive grew. I became a cheerleader for the rescue efforts.

Lady Luck arrived in the 11th hour to help out the Wild Boars. Her timing couldn't have been more dramatic. I saw a miracle firsthand. I marveled at the bravery of the British cave divers. I prayed that no harm would come to any of the divers. Many more would need to make that treacherous trip in order to get the boys safely out of the cave.

Chapter 14

With the arrival of the British cave divers, our situation changed drastically. Ton had been on the verge of an atrocious murder. Now, unable to complete his wicked act, his frustration escalated to an entirely new plane. Exasperated to the point of exploding, Ton flew around wildly in a rage most of the time. It would be impossible to reason with him. Ton acted unpredictably. He'd snapped. I found myself in a sleeping chamber with a crazy ghost and two family members who were against my Dad and me. Time was running out.

The five of us ghosts wasted most of the morning of July 3rd sitting around on our asses, discussing things, and wondering what to do. Ton became so irritated that it caused him physical problems, and a twitch developed underneath one of his eyes. His hunger needed to be satisfied, and he became completely unstable. Ton's short fuse would ignite at any moment.

The Wild Boars had been trapped in the cave for 11 days. They all wanted to get out as quickly as possible. In contrast, our group had been trapped here for centuries. Like a prisoner who has been locked up for too long, I wasn't sure that any one of us wanted to be released. I wasn't sure if we could have handled the outside world. Would I ever get a chance to know?

♦ ♦ ♦ ♦ ♦

In Chamber 3 what were the military experts and leaders thinking? Would they risk more diving in the cave? In order to keep the Wild Boars alive, they would need to bring in food and other provisions soon. Given the huge initial risks taken to locate the boys, I felt certain that more divers would keep coming.

Somehow the divers must have come to grips with the awful danger of their mission. Dwelling on fear and worst-case scenarios would lead to inaction. Navy SEALs are trained to evaluate risks, engage, and take action. They control their fears. I guessed that the rescuers simply cast aside the danger of the mission for the sake of the Wild Boars.

Would the well-trained Thai Navy SEALs go all the way to Diving Board? Could they rig some sort of oxygen-providing hose up in there? Pump out the cave? Bring in supplies? How much longer would the rains continue unabated? When would the first Wild Boar die? The situation was a mess—a real, fucking mess. I didn't have the answers; I suspected that no one did. Our conversation continued. Uncle Moo and Nid seemed to have sobered up a bit.

"Is there any chance that divers could go past the boys and reach our chamber?" Ton asked.

"It's a possibility, but highly unlikely," I said.

"What about coming in from the other side of the cave?" Uncle Moo asked.

"No, I don't think so. That would be four miles farther. The conditions there are probably even worse," my Dad said.

"There's no shorter way in?" my brother asked.

"If there were, I think the soldiers would have found it by now," I said.

"We would have found it by now," my Dad said.

"There are no secret passages for humans. She made sure of it," Ton said.

"Yeah, figures," I said.

"Kla, you better keep maintaining your lookout," Ton said.

"I think that I should go back to Diving Board and see what's happening there," I said.

"Okay, Uan," Ton said.

"My head hurts," my brother said.

"Mine, too," Uncle Moo said.

"Why don't you guys stay here then? I'll report back as usual," I said.

"Fine. Fine by me," Nid said.

"Okay," Uncle Moo said.

"Nid, Moo, and I will stay here," Ton said.

That statement was the first rational thing to come out of Ton's mouth in a while. I felt relieved that he would stay behind with the others.

My curiosity about the Wild Boars was piqued. I needed to go back and see what they were doing. I felt sure that they would be more active today. I'd been observing a mass of lifeless bodies, but now new life had been breathed into them. What were the boys like? How were they reacting to being discovered? Would they be talking more? Moving around more? How had hope changed them? I felt a burning desire to know.

"I'm taking off," I said.

"Good luck, Uan," Uncle Moo said.

"Don't let any cave divers see you," Ton said.

"Use caution," my brother said.

"They might bring in some sacred orange cloth to wrap the boys in and protect them from us. Watch yourself!" Ton said.

"Yeah, take extreme care," Uncle Moo said.

"Where's the bottle?" my brother asked. "I need a drink."

"Me, too," Uncle Moo said.

"We'll need to open another," Ton said.

I knew that Ton, Uncle Moo, and Nid planned to drink all day. At least they wouldn't be active in the cave. I never asked Ton where the Maker's Mark came from and I hoped that his supply wouldn't run out. Drinking kept those guys occupied.

My Dad resumed his sentry position while I flew off toward Diving Board. I made the difficult passage without incident. When I approached the boys this time, several of them were up taking a drink. I assumed a hover position from where I could watch the area in which the British cave divers had emerged. I listened to the boys. They spoke a lot more now that they'd been granted a second chance.

"Do you think they're coming back?"

"Yes, if it's possible."

"He promised us."

"I believed him."

"I did, too."

"Me, too."

"We'll be rescued for sure."

"Yeah."

"I'm hungrier now than ever."

"That's because you think you'll be getting more food today."

"Your desire."

"When you knew you wouldn't be getting any food, you didn't hope for it. Now that there's hope, you desire food. You're hungrier."

"In Buddhism we learn not to desire things. If you have no desires, you have no expectations. With no expectations your mind can be relaxed."

"Free from thoughts?"

"Yes in a way."

"So I shouldn't think about wanting food?"

"If you try to do that, you're thinking about food. You must let the thoughts naturally wash out of your mind. Through meditation you can clear your mind. When that happens, your desires will gradually disappear on their own. Your mind will be blank."

"His mind is always blank."

"Ha-ha-ha."

"I'm serious."

"So am I."

"Enough joking."

"So, if we didn't have that trickle of water there waiting for us to drink from, we probably wouldn't get as thirsty?"

"That's right."

"I think he's got a point."

"When I ride my bicycle a long distance in the heat, I prefer to have an empty water bottle rather than one that only contains a single sip remaining. If there's a sip left, I have to think about when to drink it. But, if it's empty, I don't have that thought. I don't have to make a decision.

"You solve a simple urge by taking the last sip. Once that last sip is gone, your problem is solved.

Mind activity quieted. A single sip doesn't make a real difference in your thirst. One remaining sip troubles your mind constantly, though."

"I see what you're saying. It's almost like a pebble in your shoe. Once it's removed, it no longer troubles you. While it's there, it's a constant bother."

"That's right."

"In our case we've had a steady trickle of drinking water."

"It's always flowed."

"So we didn't have to worry about using the last sip."

"We knew that if we needed a drink, we always could get one. We didn't face the sip dilemma."

"That's right again."

I marveled at the conversation. The boys had become young philosophers. Meditation was a good thing for them. I could see how much the Wild Boars had grown up in the past two weeks. They'd been forced to accelerate the individual learning process in order to survive. Being trapped and blinded in complete darkness had given them a perfect classroom for learning. Nothing distracted them. They'd acquired a tremendous education.

Having no choice but to cope with their situation, the Wild Boars, well, had learned to cope. Anyone who was in such a situation and could maintain his sanity would have learned to cope. It was in the nature and survival instincts of humans to adapt. Ton didn't maintain his sanity, and he couldn't cope.

When forced to confront a brutal situation or environment, humans had no choice but to work through that issue. And over millions of years and generations only those who survived, only the strongest, passed on their DNA. The ones who couldn't adapt and adjust, the weak, succumbed. Some of these boys must have been hill-tribe people or had immediate ancestors who were. Hill-tribe people are the strongest people and have survived everything.

When the boys' conversation died down, my mind settled a bit. I only now noticed that I'd been tightly gripping a stalactite. I released it. I thought of the woman in the purple blouse. In a strange way she gave me hope. Now that I had hope, I desired her. That desire made me feel uneasy.

A desire which can't be satisfied is indeed troubling. Oh, screw it, I would suffer the consequences of thinking about her. The pleasure that her beauty brought to me was worth the suffering. Well worth it. I would continue to offer myself glimpses of her beauty. I wouldn't pour her out of my mind. I never would drink the last sip of her.

"Look, a light!"

"A light! A light!"

"Divers!"

"More divers!"

"They're back!"

"Like they promised!"

"Same guys?"

I, too, saw a faint light. The light slowly grew brighter following a channel. I grabbed my stalactite again. Soon a couple of cave divers came splashing out of the murk. As they stood up, muddy water flowed off of them onto the pool's edge and ran back down. The divers scanned the area with their headlamps and lights. Some of the boys shielded their eyes. I could see a lot of white teeth. The divers reached up and removed their regulators and masks.

"Sa waa dii krap!"

Thai Navy SEALs greeted the Wild Boars! The faces on the boys lit up. More hope. Great hope. Unparalleled hope. The reality of being in Thailand and the hope of being safe again crashed over the boys like a tsunami of euphoria. I barely refrained from screaming with joy: hooray, hooray, hooray!

"Hi!"

"Hi!"

...

"Hi!"

"Hi!"

Every single boy said 'hi' and one of the divers gave him a personal 'hi' back. Marvelous smiles emerged on everyone's faces. Utmost joy and excitement. That greeting showed me why the divers had risked it all. That moment made their risks worth it—to be part of the purest joy and kindness.

To serve strangers so freely, it was the best that humanity has to offer.

And, I now understood better why in some cultures throughout the world it is an honor to welcome strangers into one's home. To assist a weary traveler, a fellow human being, is pure brotherhood. Unconditional giving from the heart is the most important thing in humanity—giving love freely when neither love nor anything else is expected in return. These divers certainly didn't expect anything back from the Wild Boars. The divers' own giving brought them tremendous fulfillment and happiness. That was all they needed.

"We've food, drinks, blankets, and medicine."

"Wow!"

"Thanks."

"Thank you so much …"

"For coming back!"

"For saving us, sir!"

"Yeah!"

"I'm so happy!"

"You've got it, boys. We're here for you."

A couple of the Wild Boars broke down. One did a jig and almost fainted. The immensity of their relief brought to the surface the boys' shattered emotions. I saw several boys embrace each other tightly, bawling uncontrollably until their energy ran out. Their love for each other was immense. The divers' human touch gave the boys new life.

Like hunters in the jungle fending off an attacking animal together, the Wild Boars saved one another. Their ability to do nothing, to sit and meditate, to wait patiently, well, that saved them, too. Even the darkness helped to save them. If the boys had been allowed to see how pitiful they truly looked, their hope might have abandoned them.

"We're going to bring you boys home. The entire world is pulling for you. You've made international news!"

"My Mom isn't going to be happy with me."

"Ha-ha-ha!"

Everyone burst into laughter. Few things in the world are as beautiful as a Thai smile.

"She'll forgive you."

"Ha-ha!"

"Here take this. You can use these wipes to clean up your backsides. We've antibiotic cream. Once you've washed your open sores, wash your hands, and apply the cream."

"Put your waste in this bag."

"Don't share the wipes. Use them only once. They're sterile."

"Here's a light."

"Wash your hands with the wipes before you eat."

"We're starving"

"I can't even imagine."

"Nothing spicy now."

"Aww."

"Ha-ha."

"Go slowly with the food. We don't want you getting sick. Your stomachs have shrunk."

"We're getting out of here?"

"We'll get you all out of here."

"Yippee, we're all going home, boys!"

Although the initial discovery by the British divers had been an amazing encounter, I felt blessed to be here when the Thai Navy SEALs made contact. It was a beautiful, extraordinary reunion of lost Thais with their compatriots. How long had I been weeping tears of joy? I only now noticed that my cheeks were dripping. I released my stalactite again fearing that I might rip it right off and attract attention.

I never imagined that I would see anything this beautiful. My imagination wasn't this good. And, I was the only spectator. Everyone else was involved in the scene, but I could put all my energies into watching the incredible drama unfold. It was at that very moment when I felt a deep loneliness. A loneliness that I never had known—a sickness crept over me. Would I need to vomit?

I felt a burning need and overwhelming urge to share this scene with someone whom I loved—my queen and soulmate. An emptiness that I never knew welled up inside of me. The void was vast. Other than my Dad, I was terribly alone.

My desire to share this scene with someone I loved sent me reeling. Feelings that I never even knew that I was capable of saturated me. I wept. Like the Wild Boars, I would need to cope with the feelings that had been forced upon me. My feelings were here now, and I would need to process and deal with them.

I felt alive. My heart could feel again. I could feel love. The cave divers had rescued me as well as the Wild Boars. Even if I died in the cave tomorrow, I felt more fulfilled at this moment than I ever had previously.

Chapter 15

The Wild Boars cleaned up. They ate some snacks. And despite their ravenous state, the boys remained polite. It wasn't just fight over it, grab, chew once, and swallow like a pack of wild dogs. They shared their food. Humans are compassionate and thoughtful, and they don't simply live by animal instincts and survival of the fittest. The boys proved that as even the weakest of them was treated equally.

The food items appeared to have been selected by a doctor. I was thankful for that. I couldn't imagine the boys putting spicy Thai food into their empty stomachs. If the boys had been given the foods that they desired, they probably wouldn't have survived. I smiled. They were still just boys.

The exceptional concern provided by the devoted Thai Navy SEALs made me feel truly blessed to be an onlooker to the situation. My emotions ran amok. The entire scene became almost too much to bear. Yesterday's initial contact and today's first contact by Thais now formed my two best memories ever.

The burning desire to share these moments with someone whom I loved still ate away at me. But I couldn't share them. My situation was bleak. Should I let go of my hope? The Wild Boars never let go of theirs. But I'm a ghost. A ghost condemned to the underground for a crime that my cousin Ton committed, and I witnessed. Trapped like the Wild Boars in the underground by being in the wrong place at the wrong time.

Life doesn't always deal you the cards that you want, but you *must* play the hand that you're dealt. The last two days had given me a renewed hope. I decided that I wouldn't let that hope die. The Wild Boars showed me a never-die attitude. The Navy SEALs showed me how to set aside fear and take action. Just like the Wild Boars, I would try to get out of the cave's stranglehold.

I'd been stuck in a cave for hundreds of years with but one good ghost, my Dad. Being imprisoned here so long without much good had stifled my growth. Similarly to the Wild Boars, I grew more in the past two weeks than I'd grown in my entire existence—one which spanned many centuries. The stimulus for that growth had been a group of lost boys. Although they didn't even know about me, they'd become my teachers.

For several hundred years I simply had accepted my fate. One that condemned me to this cave because a rich and powerful man didn't want his daughter, a princess, to marry a common man—a man with whom the princess was deeply in love and a man who loved her unconditionally. Thanks to the Wild Boars, I saw the possibility of questioning my fate for the very first time ever.

I recalled my past. On that fateful day so long ago in the hills of Chiang Rai, Ton gathered my Dad, Uncle Moo, Nid, and me. Ton had been hired by the princess's father to kill her common-man lover to ensure that she wouldn't elope and marry him—a man who could only afford a small dowry. Marrying below her class wasn't acceptable to her rich father. He would do anything to prevent such a marriage.

Ton planned to kill an innocent man for a meager sum of money. Human greed is a nasty condition. It got us all into trouble. Drafted as Ton's soldiers, the five of us followed the common man into the hills one day. There he picked a bouquet of flowers for his princess.

At the time I wasn't much older than the members of the Wild Boars. I went along for the ride. It was something to do that weekend. I didn't comprehend the gravity of the situation. At my age I couldn't comprehend a love as deep as the one the princess felt for her common man. I knew nothing about life or death.

I didn't know a thing about society's classes. The details of the princess's situation hadn't been explained to me. I didn't know the common man was innocent. His only crime had been to fall in love with a princess—a woman deeply devoted to him.

Ton ambushed the man. Ton struck him in the back of the head with a fallen tree branch. As the poor man fell, he dropped his bouquet and clutched his head. Uncle Moo and Nid pounced and held the poor man down while Ton stabbed him to death in a bloody scene. Blood squirted everywhere from the wounds. Ton's face and arms turned red. Blood splashed all over Uncle Moo and Nid. They wiped at their faces and spit out blood that entered their mouths.

My Dad and I watched in shocked horror. Things happened quickly. I made a gesture to assist the poor common man. I couldn't just stand by and witness his murder. The common man saw me and reached in my direction, perhaps his last moment of hope. My Dad saved my life by restraining me, as Ton surely would have killed me if I became involved.

Only just now did I realize that in saving me on that fateful day, my Dad actually had ended my life. I committed a terrible crime by giving a dying man hope and then taking that hope away. I committed a crime against a fellow man in need of help by watching him be murdered. I could have tried harder to save the common man. I didn't serve him as well as the cave divers had served the Wild

Boars. They were much better men than I. My life had been wasted.

At the murder scene Ton became a crazed madman repeatedly stabbing the innocent common man even after the man bled to death. To all of our horror, the princess herself had witnessed her lover's murder. Unbeknownst to us, she'd followed us into the jungle's hills. I never forgot the speed at which the princess ran toward Ton that day.

Ton's knife was still in the heart of the dead man. The princess slapped Ton's bloody face throwing him off balance. Uncle Moo and Nid jumped back not wanting to feel her wrath. What would the princess do? She moved quickly. She fulfilled her plan.

"My father did this. He won't have me. You'll all pay for this horrible murder, you bastards!" the princess shouted.

Ton looked on in a state of shock while still reeling. Blood covered the ground. Ton's anger toward the princess built. In one felled swoop the princess pulled the knife out of her lover's heart and thrust the bloody weapon into her own heart, joining her lover's heart to hers. Sharing their blood.

As the princess twisted the knife, she gasped, "You'll all rot in hell! I love you, my Darling!"

Ton grabbed the bloody knife handle and yanked it from the princess's chest.

"Bitch!" He screamed. "Look what you've done!"

Suddenly the earth savagely opened up before our eyes—a massive upheaval on the scale such as when the earth was formed. I grabbed my Dad. The earth trembled angrily and the surrounding hills transformed into mountains in the shape of the princess. We fell spinning wildly out of control through the earth. I vomited repeatedly during the free fall. We landed in the princess's stomach.

A great cave formed in response to her suicide. We would pay for our crime against the princess's lover by being imprisoned here. Our fear, the princess's action, the forces of good, and our fall to the underground transformed us into milky white ghosts. When the great shaking and earth movements finally settled, the five of us sat in the Tham Luang Cave in the middle of the Mountain of the Sleeping Lady—the princess's mountain.

Ton clutched his knife. It was the only item from above ground that accompanied us into the underground. Condemned forever, we were trapped in the princess's stomach. The fear that we'd felt that day and the supernatural powers of the princess that we'd been subject to stunned us so mightily that I'm sure none of us had ever even questioned if we could break her spell. Up until now, I felt my fate had been sealed.

Although the Wild Boars seemed on the verge of sharing my fate, they never had accepted it. They never completely felt doomed. They never gave up their hope of returning from the underground. The boys hung onto their dreams. They had shown me that I could question my own fate. I now did question my fate. The Wild Boars helped me to ask a question that I never even had conceived of on my own. Could I somehow escape from the cave? From my destiny? And, if it were possible, how?

But the Wild Boars were different. They came into the cave voluntarily. Or had they? Had the princess lured them here and trapped them? From their darkness the Wild Boars opened my eyes and my mind.

◆ ◆ ◆ ◆ ◆

The Wild Boars and cave divers gave me a new hope and faith. I'd waited patiently in the cave too long. I never thought that I'd been waiting to see the light. I never thought of escaping my doom, but now that thought overwhelmed me. I saw how beautiful life could be. I wanted to get out of my dungeon. If I saw an escape, I would take it. Ready or not to re-enter society, I wanted out. Seeing the great risks that the cave divers took gave me the courage to risk it all. If I died trying to get out of the cave, it was worth the risk.

Some rescuers might die trying to get into the cave in the name of service, coming to the aid of total strangers. Their heroism changed my attitude toward many things. A life in unbreakable chains was no longer worth living. It was no life at all. I would be better off with a single moment of freedom rather than spending my remaining days here. I wanted to see the outside world. I needed to see the outside world. Thank you, Wild Boars! Thank you, cave divers!

Chapter 16

After the short trip back to the sleeping chamber, I gave my report to the others. I didn't bother to fill them in on all of the things that had been troubling my mind and about my new personal resolution. Instead, I let them know that Thai Navy SEALs reached the boys and gave them food, blankets, drinks, lights, and medicine. I told my companions that the boys seemed to be getting a bit stronger.

Ton remained in his foul mood. I could see his evil mind working, as I described the state of the boys. Fortunately, the alcohol slowed down his thought process. He looked tired and could barely respond. Nid and Uncle Moo also appeared exhausted. This ordeal drained everyone. With my new lease on life providing me a burst of energy, I kept talking for a while, but soon the three alcoholics fell asleep.

When my Dad and I were alone, my Dad said, "Uan, you seem different. You seem to have changed."

"I have, Dad. I'm a new person. I'm getting out of here," I said.

"But, you're not a person at all. You're a ghost, Uan," my Dad said.

"I disagree, Dad. The Wild Boars have given me a great new hope. I'm sure that I can get out of here someday," I said.

My Dad nodded in agreement even though he didn't believe me.

"You're crying," my Dad said.

"Can't help it," I said.

My Dad didn't want me to be disappointed. He saw my conviction. I understood my Dad's limitations. I only had just overcome those same limitations myself. Just as it had been for the Wild Boars, this day had been an extremely important one for me. My Dad was right. I had changed.

There wasn't anything left to say, so my Dad and I decided to go to sleep as well. On that evening of July 3rd, as my head rested on my pillow, thoughts of the woman in the purple blouse continued to float around in my head. I couldn't place her face, but now, more than ever, I was certain that I'd seen it somewhere before.

On July 4th the five of us ghosts sat around talking about the situation in the cave. Uncle Moo, Nid, and Ton were passing a fresh bottle of Maker's

Mark around. They still seemed coherent, but if the drinking continued at this rate, I knew that they would all soon be three sheets to the wind.

"What the fuck was that?" Ton asked.

"You felt it, too?" Uncle Moo asked.

"Yeah, you dope, it's not just you!" Ton said.

"Those are vibrations. From drilling?" my Dad said.

"Drilling?" my brother asked.

"Listen!" Ton said.

"It's got to be drilling!" my Dad said.

"The bastards are going to drill a hole through to the boys!" Ton said.

"Once they knew roughly where the boys were in the cave, they probably used a beacon to pinpoint their exact location," my Dad said.

"And ours!" Ton said.

"We're about a half mile beneath bedrock here," my Dad said.

"They'll drill down here to get the boys out. Get them out using brute force. Drop in a long line or send in some climbers," Uncle Moo said.

"I don't think they can drill a hole that wide and that deep," I said.

"Maybe they're just trying to get more oxygen in to the boys. To keep them alive until they can rescue them by some other means," my Dad said.

"Wouldn't drill holes fill up with water and cause more flooding?" my brother asked.

"How the fuck do I know? I'm not an engineer. That'd be a question for a guy like Elon Musk, not me," Ton said.

"You mean the South African billionaire?" my brother asked.

"Yeah, the genius from Pretoria. Electronic cars, space travel. All that shit," Ton said.

"He's probably got some good ideas on how to get the boys out," my Dad said.

"Like what, a mini kid's submarine or something?" Uncle Moo asked.

"Ha-ha-ha," Ton and my brother burst into laughter.

"Oh, forget it. Musk's a good guy, and I'm sure that he'd be willing to help the boys however he could," I said.

"If they drill a hole into this chamber, we're all fucked," Ton said.

"Damn right we are!" Uncle Moo said.

The deliberations about our predicament continued. No satisfactory solutions came to us. Should we go deeper into the cave? Move our sleeping chamber? End my recon missions? Of course, none of us had faced any situation even remotely like this in the past.

Things happened quickly. One day British cave divers appeared on our doorstep and the next day Thai Navy SEALs. Today people drilled into our sleeping chamber. I'd questioned my fate. What other surprises awaited us in the near future?

"We can't just sit around here and do nothing," Ton said.

"You mean like those Wild Boars," Uncle Moo said.

"Yes, I mean like those Wild Boars!" Ton said.

"What do you suggest?" Uncle Moo asked.

"Well, we need to find out what these rescuers are planning," my Dad intervened.

"Uan, you've been the one doing all the recon missions. Today I want you to take Moo and Nid along, too. Go out near the cave's entrance. We need more eyes and ears. Maybe you missed something. Something important," Ton said.

"That'd be very dangerous. Maybe even a suicide mission," I said.

"Nid and Moo are going with you today," Ton stated emphatically.

Ton, Uncle Moo, and Nid had been on a drinking binge ever since the Wild Boars became stuck in the cave. Being drunk allowed them to cope with and forget our problems. I understood that at a certain level, but I didn't want to go on a spectacularly dangerous mission with two guys who'd been badly hungover all week. Although not yet sloshed, they already had been drinking again today.

"That's probably not a good idea, Ton. The journey is very tough and in their physical condition I'm not sure they can make it," my Dad offered.

"Don't be silly," Nid said. "I fine. I fine."

"Me, too. Me, too," Uncle Moo repeated himself.

"Really?" I asked.

"Don't worry about Nid, Uan. If you can make it, he can make it. If he can make it, I can make it," Uncle Moo said.

What kind of transitive logic was Uncle Moo throwing at me? It didn't make any sense. I didn't see any alternatives.

"All right, Ton. If you guys insist," I said.

"Yeah, we insist," Ton said.

"Yeah, we do," Uncle Moo and Nid said together.

"Okay. It's settled," I said.

My Dad and I both recognized that Nid and Uncle Moo joining me spelled trouble. Big trouble. But there was little that we could do to stop them. Ton demanded that the two accompany me. I figured Ton didn't want to travel himself because he deeply feared encountering an Orange. He feared the Orange more than anything else in the world. Ton feared death more than any of us. In a warped way he may have felt that killing a man gave him more life.

While Nid and Uncle Moo continued drinking, I made a few preparations.

"You ready, Nid? Uncle Moo?" I inquired after a spell.

"Yeah," my brother said.

"Yup," Uncle Moo said.

"Okay, let's go, guys," I said.

"Be careful, son," my Dad said.

My Dad moved toward his sentry position. Uncle Moo and Nid hovered. Ton continued drinking and gave some final instructions.

"Keep an eye out, Nid. Moo. Ears and eyes, huh?" Ton said.

"Sure, Ton," Uncle Moo said.

"Yes, sir!" Nid said.

The three of us flew slowly toward my Dad.

"Probably best if you two follow me. I know the way. Keep quiet. If I raise my hand, stop. If I lower my hand, back up slowly. Silence at all times," I said.

"Don't be so uptight, Uan," Nid said.

"Yeah, Uan. We know what we're doing," Uncle Moo said.

"Okay," I said.

"Okay, okay," Uncle Moo said.

"You sure that you're both sober enough? We can do this tomorrow after you dry out," I said.

"I fine. I fine," Nid said.

"Never felt better," Uncle Moo said.

"Let's do this," I said.

With that simple instruction and check, my brother, Uncle Moo, and I flew off together in formation.

Chapter 17

I'd been tracing the same route daily since the Wild Boars became trapped. One might think that I simply followed the exact same passage every day, but with the changing water levels and currents, I often needed to get creative and alter my path. The detours helped me to stay more alert and avoid getting lulled into letting my guard down. I often found my head underwater and several times nearly drowned.

Each time that I saw the Wild Boars I felt terribly sad. I could tell that the poor boys were dying. The life was being sucked right out of them. Somehow, against all odds, they always seemed to maintain a modicum of hope of exiting the cave. After being found by the British cave divers and then being revisited by the Thai Navy SEALs, that hope only grew.

Although the provisions given to the Wild Boars by the Thai Navy SEALs slowed down the boys' rate of deterioration, death still seemed to be knocking on their door. The oxygen level in the

Diving Board area probably had dropped to a mere 15 percent. The air that the boys were breathing was poisonous. While staring into the face of death, where did the boys' powerful faith come from? The Wild Boars believed in themselves more than anyone reasonably could have. Did they ever lose any soccer games? I smiled.

Love among the boys and thoughts of their families must have somehow kept them going. The assistant coach found a way to keep them calm. He taught them how to meditate. The boys must have trusted him completely. Given that he was an authority figure and probably ten years older than the oldest boy, I'm sure that the boys looked up to and respected him. Having a strong leader was important to their survival.

The situation with the Wild Boars became so tragic that I held a personal moment of silence on their behalf each time that I visited. Many times I teared up when I saw the boys. Like an old reliable dog that just won't die, they suffered terribly. My stomach ached. I prayed that the visits from the cave divers hadn't merely given the boys false hopes.

Nid and Uncle Moo traveled with me, and I needed to keep a close eye on those two clowns. I didn't like that they both had throbbing headaches. I didn't like that at all. When I flew alone, I made much-better time. I really felt powerless to do anything, though, as Ton, and even they themselves insisted on going with me.

At last Nid, Uncle Moo, and I approached the ledge where the boys rested. Occasionally, my brother bumped me from behind. Dammit! Nid flew too close. Way too close. I also heard him make contact with the ceiling a few times. Sober up, Nid. Uncle Moo seemed a bit more controlled. His constant belching annoyed the hell out of me, though.

"We're nearing the boys, guys. Move quietly. Deliberately," I said.

"Burrrrp."

"Yeah, yeah," Nid said.

"Burrrp, burrrrrrp …"

"Uncle Moo," I said.

For almost two weeks Nid and Uncle Moo had heard me report about the boys, but they never had seen the Wild Boars in person. How would they react? The three of us hovered side-by-side. We reached the boys and stared down at them. Thin and dirty, the Wild Boars were a pitiful sight. I turned to see my brother raise a hand over his mouth. The boys' tragic situation even touched Nid. I raised a finger to my lips. I could tell that my brother wanted to speak, but I successfully stopped him.

Uncle Moo simply shook his head from side to side. I noticed tears welling up in his eyes. Luckily, he wasn't positioned directly over anyone. Uncle

Moo attempted to share his thoughts, but I stopped him too before he could make a sound. This time I wondered if the boys might be sleeping better. The medicines reduced their skin irritations and pain, and the food probably settled their stomachs.

I took some comfort in realizing that at a minimum people would know the location where the Wild Boars all died and that they all died in peace surrounded by their best friends. The thought of dying and never being found is a tough concept for humans to accept. The uncertainty that would remain for those above ground would be unbearable. The lack of finality would be an ongoing torture for their families and friends.

Since the boys were all sleeping soundly, the three of us moved farther along. When we flew and wiggled our way through a few tight spots a distance from the Wild Boars, I signaled Nid and Uncle Moo to stop. Nid slammed right into me.

"Didn't you see my hand?" I asked.

"Obviously not," Nid said.

"Pay attention!" I said.

"Pay attention," Nid echoed back sarcastically.

"Ha-ha-ha, burrrp …," Uncle Moo laughed.

Sweat poured off Nid's forehead. Uncle Moo breathed hard. His burping continued without pause. We finally had a chance to talk.

"My head hurts. Oh, those poor boys," Uncle Moo said.

"Yeah, they're so damn helpless. So thin," Nid said.

I could tell that the predicament of the boys troubled my brother and Uncle Moo. Now that they'd observed the Wild Boars firsthand, they felt differently about the boys. Unlike Ton, they felt compassion.

"If the boys don't get rescued soon, I'm afraid they'll all die," I said.

"Poor fellows. They look terrible. Burp, burrrrrp. And the smell in that chamber was horrendous," Uncle Moo said.

"Like your breath. I almost vomited," my brother said.

"Imagine their suffering, Nid. Think about it, Uncle Moo. They're just boys," I said.

"Prisoners like us. Trapped," my brother said.

"Not just like us, but yes, prisoners," I said.

"Trapped here somehow. Burrrrp," Uncle Moo said.

Once our conversation petered out, the three of us decided to push on toward the mouth of the cave, or at least until we encountered some more cave divers. I could see that my two companions felt deeply troubled. I worried about their concentration levels. Neither one seemed to be himself. I would do my best to keep a close eye on the two.

Uncle Moo, Nid, and I reached Pattaya Beach without any major incident. I didn't really appreciate my brother's poor flying skills, though. A bit farther along I could see that the water level around Upside-Down Shark's Fin had dropped appreciably. Were the men pumping out the cave? I speculated that the machines and hoses which I'd seen were probably all in use now. I listened carefully, but I couldn't hear any pumps. What else could explain the lower water level? I believed that it was still raining.

"Burrrrp."

I almost had drowned in this exact spot on more than one occasion. Those incidents had led me to take the Laawt Yaow route. I'd taken that route on all of my recons ever since Upside-Down Shark's Fin had flooded completely. I preferred that way now. Although much longer and tedious, it seemed much-less hazardous.

"Guys, let's go up here to Laawt Yaow. It's not safe to go under Upside-Down Shark's Fin," I said.

"I hate Laawt Yaow. We need to vaporize," Nid said.

"Yeah, then reintegrate. I don't want to do that with my headache. That'll take forever. Burrrrp. Burp," Uncle Moo said.

"I've been using that route almost every day for about a week," I said.

"Why take it, Uan? Look at the gap there. This'll work just fine. Go under the Fin," my brother said.

Nid pointed in the direction of Upside-Down Shark's Fin. I could see an air gap. Was there a gap even at the very tip of the fin? One couldn't tell from here.

"If you don't want to go with us, take Laawt Yaow. We'll wait for you on the other side," my brother said.

"Burrp. What are you afraid of, Uan? Burrrrp," Uncle Moo said.

"If you two insist. I'll follow behind you. Watch yourself, Nid. If the water level rises suddenly, this will be tricky. Strong current," I said.

"I fine. I fine," my brother said.

"Burrrrp," Uncle Moo's belching continued.

"Follow me, Moo. I want to lead," my brother said.

"Nid, that's not a good idea," I said.

In spite of my warning, fearless Nid forged ahead with Uncle Moo trailing closely behind. They were both slightly buzzed and hungover. Seeing the Wild Boars in a pile impacted my brother profoundly. Distracted and emotional, Nid moved forward without any regard for his own personal safety. The cave divers had traversed Upside-Down Shark's Fin in both directions. Facing that section now, I admired their enormous bravery and courage.

Cave divers are trained to think clearly and make good decisions when under extreme duress. Cave divers are methodical and detailed. They only take calculated risks and have redundant pieces of gear in case a vital instrument fails. Nid and Uncle

Moo had no business being here. They weren't qualified for anything except drinking.

I watched Uncle Moo bumbling along behind my brother. To my great surprise we made steady progress underneath Upside-Down Shark's Fin. Maybe the guys were right. I followed a safe distance behind Uncle Moo and occasionally would lose sight of him. Suddenly, a violent surge and big wave of murky water threw me backward.

"Shit! Shit! No!" I screamed.

Had the workers pumped water into the cave instead of out of it? Did the drilling open new avenues for water to flood the cave? No time to think. Emergency! I turned and flew at full throttle in the shrinking air gap. I could see the water level rising and almost touching my chest. Fly! Fly! I encouraged myself. This is going to be tight! I made it out and flipped once before a hard landing on the rocks. I rolled over. What about my brother and Uncle Moo?

I stood up and stared at the rising, rushing water. Vertigo set in instantly. I glanced up briefly. In my dizzying state I saw Uncle Moo's flailing arms. His head bobbed up momentarily and then dipped under the powerful, murky water. Uncle Moo's body washed past me. He hadn't made it out before the air gap flooded. I knew that his lungs had filled with water. Seconds later Nid floated by me face down. The force of the water sucked him under. Then Nid's head popped up.

"Help me!" my brother yelled.

"Nid! Nid, grab my hand!" I called.

I thrust out my hand to save my brother. He couldn't see me; he couldn't see my hand. Nid's ears were underwater, and I don't think that he heard me calling.

"Nid! Nid, take my hand! Come on!" I yelled.

I didn't have much time before I lost him for good. I recklessly lunged farther in my brother's direction, and I almost fell into the turbid water myself. I glanced up to fight off my vertigo.

"Fuck! Nid! Nid! Grab me!" I screamed.

I saw my brother getting pulled down in a thrashing vortex. The brown water bubbled. Searching for a handhold, I tried to secure myself to part of the cave's wall. I filled my lungs with air. I submerged my head in the water and felt a great tug on the back of my neck. As my head oscillated back and forth from the pounding current, my grip on the rock loosened. No! The flesh on my fingers ripped off, as I slipped.

I felt Nid's wrist brush over my submerged hand's fingertips. Thank God. Then instantly my brother disappeared. I'd missed gripping his wrist. The muddy vortex dragged my brother beneath the surface. Silty water splashed all over my face. I rapidly blinked my eyes and spit. With my strength ebbing I made a last-ditch effort to pull myself out of the water. Down to my final breath, I jerked myself upward and onto a patch of rocky cave floor.

"Oh, shit! Niiiidddddd …," I said.

Nid was gone; my brother had drowned. What about Uncle Moo? I forced myself back up to search for him. I called, but no reply came. Uncle Moo drowned, too. I rolled onto my back on the rocks, chest heaving. I spit out some sandy water. Rubbed my eyes.

I lay on the rocks for some time thinking about my brother. I was sorry that our relationship hadn't been a better one. I was sorry that I never could help patch things up between my brother and father. And Uncle Moo was gone, too. It all happened so suddenly. I didn't shed a tear, as I had done for the Wild Boars. But the loss of Nid and Uncle Moo at the same time troubled me deeply.

I trembled. Should I head back now? Or, push on with my recon alone? Would I make a stupid mistake in my emotional condition? I needed to report the terrible drownings of Nid and Uncle Moo to my Dad and Ton. Ton would be angry as hell. I didn't know how my Dad would react.

The adrenaline rush caused by attempting to save my brother's life had drained me completely. How long had I been on the rocks? Did I pass out? I decided that I should continue my recon. There had been a lot of activity since the other day: drilling, pumping out and perhaps accidently flooding the cave, planning, and who knows what else. I steadied myself and moved off the rocks. Be careful, Uan. Nid and Uncle Moo are gone.

Chapter 18

After the deaths of Nid and Uncle Moo on July 4th, I traversed Laawt Yaow, made my way up a muddy incline, and turned right at Sam Yak. I slogged toward the third chamber of the cave alone. What I saw blew my mind. A full-scale rescue-operations center had been set up. The number of military personnel present had swelled enormously. There must have been hundreds of people there.

I immediately recognized an American military contingent of about 30 men. I hid myself and remained quiet. From the conversations that I was able to make out, I learned that more cave divers arrived at the scene, too. A giant pile of scuba tanks indicated that many more divers would be going in the turbulent, low-visibility water. Was that an air compressor to refill tanks? The rescue mission took on war-like proportions.

The flooding in the cave continued and may have even worsened. I guessed that there were many personnel out near Chamber 1 and the mouth of the cave. Based on the number of people whom I saw, I imagined that the story of the Wild Boars had gone viral.

My home became international news. If Ton learned about the immensity of the rescue mission, he might want to make a strike in order to gain publicity. If the Wild Boars had found their way out of the cave that first night none of this would have happened. If the Wild Boars hadn't come in here during monsoon season they wouldn't have been trapped. But, they had.

I knew that many lives were in grave danger. With no real sign of letup in the rain, the conditions in the cave would only worsen. Still, the perch on which the boys were stranded probably wouldn't flood for quite some time. The poor lads couldn't hold out there much longer, though. If it hadn't been for the provisions brought in by the cave divers, the Wild Boars would have succumbed already. Could I keep making these scouting trips without additional dire consequences? Would Ton murder someone? Was our sleeping chamber safe?

While contemplating such questions, I spotted a charismatic and handsome Thai diver. He looked like an endurance athlete and moved with great poise. Others seemed to gravitate around him. He stood out among the rest. Was he a Thai Navy SEAL? Was he here as part of a Thai government rescue team? When did he arrive?

Luckily for me, a reporter approached the handsome man at just that moment. I positioned myself so that I could listen to the interview. The reporter fired questions at the man. Unfortunately, I completely missed the diver's name. Let me respectfully call him 'SEA' representing the first part of SEAL—**SE**a, **A**ir, and Land. I listened for a while and here is what I learned about SEA and the rescue mission.

As soon as SEA became aware of the plight of the Wild Boars, he grabbed the first available flight to Chiang Rai. He felt a calling to assist the boys. SEA had served as a Thai Navy SEAL, but he retired recently to spend more time with his wife and family. He volunteered to help find the Wild Boars and promised to stay around until they were safe.

SEA was an experienced technical diver and would help stage tanks for other divers. He would haul extra oxygen cylinders into the cave and position them so that returning divers could swap out tanks that were running low on air. This way the returning divers would have plenty of air to exit the water safely. If the rescue involved the boys using scuba equipment, they, too, could use the tanks that SEA would place.

I couldn't help but marvel at SEA's grace and good nature in answering questions. He was clearly in his element. His humble demeanor and ability to explain the situation in layman's terms to the reporter amazed me. SEA's rigorous training allowed him to take a practical, let's-get-this-done, positive approach to extracting the boys. Only with such confidence and expertise could one proceed with a level head while facing the unknown and essentially impossible odds.

I immediately took a strong liking to SEA—from his good looks, to his willingness to work in the service of others, to his kind and humble nature, to his leadership skills. SEA had it all and seemed like a great guy. I felt glad that SEA was around. SEA firmly believed that the Wild Boars would all get out of the Tham Luang Cave safely. His positive outlook gave me a renewed hope that the boys would be saved.

Due to the failing health of the Wild Boars, the failed attempts with drilling, the unsuccessful efforts to pump out the cave, and continued heavy rainfall, I learned that the final rescue plan involved training the boys to use scuba equipment. They would be taken out individually with two divers assisting each boy. The training of the boys to use scuba gear was underway now. That meant cave divers probably instructed the boys at this very moment. The divers must have made their way through Upside-Down Shark's Fin while I was traversing through Laawt Yaow.

Here's what I remember of SEA and the reporter's conversation, as the interview drew to a close.

"When I was a frogman, I trained for this type of mission. I trained hard with my brothers. Frogmen. I'm here to help the Wild Boars and their families. We'll bring the boys back home safely. We'll care for them. There are a lot of great people here and we're all cooperating, all working as a unit to do what we can to save lives.

"Although the conditions in the cave aren't good, we'll do what we need to do to make sure that the boys get out safely. The lives of the boys are our number one priority. No man left behind we say in the SEALs. They must all live," SEA said.

"Thanks. Thanks, that's very helpful. I appreciate your valuable time," the reporter said.

"You're welcome," SEA said.

"Good luck and be safe!" the reporter said.

"Always," SEA smiled his beautiful smile.

When the interview concluded, SEA put his palms together in front of his chest and bowed to the reporter. The reporter gave SEA a Wai in return. SEA patted the reporter on the back. I watched the reporter as he headed in the direction of the cave's entrance.

SEA resumed his work. He moved with ease and great agility. I studied him for a while placing his BCD (buoyancy control device) on one of the steel cylinders. I saw him tighten the straps on his mask. SEA tested his torches. He made a careful inspection of all of his dive gear. I admired SEA's faith and his never-die attitude. It refreshed me to see a man who was so strong and full of life.

Watching such a talented and skilled man at work almost made me forget who I was and what I

Raymond Greenlaw

was doing. I needed to get back to my Dad and Ton. I needed to break the bad news to them. As I turned to head back through the cave, she appeared again. The woman in the purple blouse stood there looking around. I'd been looking for her for nine days.

I stared at the beautiful lady with my mouth agape. Where had she been? Who was she? What was her name? Was she single? Her face seemed familiar. And then, just like that, the woman with the looks of a model reversed direction and disappeared from my sight. I felt happy to have seen her again. Although I tried hard to find her, she'd vanished like a ghost. I scratched my head.

I started back again, and this time no interruptions delayed me. Along the way I would figure out how to explain Nid and Uncle Moo's deaths to my Dad and Ton. I knew that my Dad would handle their losses far better than Ton.

Chapter 19

As I weaved my way carefully through the cave's passageways, my energy level dipped to a record low. I still had a long distance to navigate before returning to my Dad's post. After winding my way through Laawt Yaow, I walked down through the mud to the spot where my brother and Uncle Moo had died. There I consumed three insect bars that I'd packed in the morning. As I chewed, I pretended that I ate the first one for my brother, the second one for Uncle Moo, and the third one for myself.

My little remembrance ceremony made me sad. A brother will always be a brother. It was hard to believe that Nid had been here with me just a short while ago. Although I tried to warn my brother and Uncle Moo, I'd failed. If we had gone underneath Upside-Down Shark's Fin a minute or two earlier, they probably would have made it. Ironically, the delay caused by my warning them may have led to their deaths. The timing had been off, just as it had been for the Wild Boars initially.

My reflections resulted in a lost half hour. The insect bars gave me an energy boost, and I fought my way back through the wet air pockets and passageways of the cave. They shrank with each passing day. I took greater risks to get back. When I reached the boys, as expected, several others occupied Diving Board as well. A doctor and a couple of Thai cave divers engaged the boys. The doctor examined the boys and administered medicine to them. The divers gave the boys scuba lessons.

I flew to my normal hover spot near my favorite stalactite. From there I watched the lessons conclude. I listened as the divers outlined a rescue plan and reviewed what they'd taught the boys while I'd been away.

"We plan to take you out individually. You'll each have two divers with you: one in front and one trailing. We'll monitor you and keep a close eye on you. No worries. We'll guide you through the cave. There's a guideline, too. You'll be tethered to a diver at all times. All you have to do is breathe normally. Due to the currents in the water, we won't be able to stop.

"When we reach an air pocket, where it's safe to stop, we'll take off your full-face mask and ask you how you're doing. Once we put your mask back on again, simply breathe normally. You'll be getting plenty of air. You'll hear your breathing and it may sound heavy, but you'll be fine. Just stay relaxed. It'll be just like we've practiced.

"The doctor may give you some medicine to help you relax. It won't hurt. No side effects. We'll monitor your air consumption. Your tanks will be full. You'll have plenty of air. All you need to do is relax.

"We'll move you along. Although you'll have a full-face mask on, the water is so murky that you might not be able to see anything. The visibility is about two inches. You may only see our lights. Dispersed light. Just remain calm. You can even close your eyes if you want. The divers with you will lead the way."

"We've been in the dark so long."

"Yeah, we'll be fine."

"Okay, boys," the dive instructor said.

Another diver continued, "The rain is continuing to fall heavily. If we get a break in the weather, we'll start taking you out of here. We'll bring in more provisions for those who are still in the cave. We're going to get you all out of here safely.

"The doctor is going to remain with you now. He'll monitor your health and needs. We'll need you a little stronger before you can make the journey out of the cave. The mission is a go."

"Be brave, boys! You'll all be home safely soon."

"Hooray! Hooray!" the Wild Boars cheered.

Unbelievable. The Thai cave divers were giving the boys a crash course in cave diving. The Wild Boars had skipped the Open Water course, the Advanced Open Water course, the Cavern Diving Course, and the Introduction to Cave Diving Course. They were jumping straight into the Full Cave Diving Course. In addition to missing all of the diving experience for Full Cave, none of the boys met the prerequisite of being over 18 years old, either. In fact, none of them could even swim!

It took pure genius to hatch this rescue plan. Only an elite diver could conceive of such an idea and believe that it actually could work. For a person with lesser skills, the idea would sound outrageous, impossible, and foolhardy—destined for grave failure. The boys were lucky indeed that they had so many well-trained technical specialists assisting them with their rescue.

As the Thai cave divers prepped to return from their mission here to the command center, I decided to head back from mine. Their day still wasn't over, and neither was mine. I'm sure that they felt extremely tired, and so did I. Once we reached our next destinations we would both face many questions. I looked back to see the divers submerge in the murky running water as I turned into the darkness of the next bend. I hoped that they would make it back safely.

Chapter 20

I felt almost faint when my Dad's position finally came into view. I held up one finger. My Dad acknowledged me and smiled. His expression displayed his happiness that I'd made the passage safely again. My Dad shrugged his shoulders as if to ask "Where are Nid and Moo?"

I flew over, and my Dad met me halfway.

"They didn't make it, Dad," I said.

I bit my lower lip. Rubbed my cheeks.

"Oh, no! Oh, nooooo!" my Dad said.

"Both of them drowned trying to go under Upside-Down Shark's Fin. A flash flood hit us there," I said.

"Oh, God!" my Dad said. "Oh, your brother."

My Dad took my hand, and the two of us flew over to where Ton sat.

"Where the fuck are Moo and Nid?" Ton asked grumpily.

I gathered myself.

"Sorry, Ton. They both drowned," I said.

"Fuck! Drowned? How?" Ton asked.

Ton stared at me. He'd reached up and placed his hands on the back of his head. His head tilted downward. Ton seemed to sober up quickly, and he listened.

"After we'd spent some time observing the boys, we left and headed past Pattaya Beach. We eventually arrived at Upside-Down Shark's Fin with no problem. Beneath it we could see a small air gap. The guys wanted to shoot the gap. I suggested that we proceed via Laawt Yaow, but they thought that route was too long. And, it did appear as if we probably could go underneath the Fin safely.

"Suddenly, the gap closed with rushing, silty, muddy water. Nid and Uncle Moo were leading. In seconds Uncle Moo washed by me. He was gone. I reached for Nid's hand as he got pulled under in a whirling vortex. The current pounded me. I felt Nid's wrist, but the muddy water blinded us both.

"Oh shit, Dad! Nid got pulled under. I never saw him again. My brother's gone! Never saw his hand break the surface. When I searched further for Uncle Moo, there wasn't any sign of him either," I said.

"It's okay, son. We know you did what you could to save them," my Dad said.

"Dammit! We've lost two good ghosts! What a big fucking shame! I don't believe this shit," Ton said.

"I tried. Believe me, I tried. It was hopeless. When that torrent hit, they didn't have a chance," I said.

"Their energy levels were down. They were both flying with hangovers," my Dad said.

"All I know is that they're both gone! Forever!" Ton said.

"We won't ever see them again. Not a drowned, dissolved ghost. The terrible suffering," I said.

"Yeah, what a painful way to go," my Dad added.

"The timing was unlucky. Just like the Wild Boars," I said.

"Yeah, just like when that bitch stabbed herself all those years ago!" Ton said.

The three of us hung our heads. Silence filled the chamber. We each remembered the fellas in our own way, I suppose. Even though my brother sided with Ton and had been a foe to my Dad and me, I still felt sorry for him, and the same with Uncle Moo. My Dad lost a son and a brother. Things hadn't turned out the way that my Dad hoped. I knew that the failed relationships troubled him dearly.

Ever since I'd been watching over the Wild Boars, my personal feelings came to the surface more often. I easily became emotional. The deaths of my brother and Uncle Moo rocked me far more than I'd anticipated. I didn't know how to cope with such feelings. I couldn't share them with anyone else in the cave.

"Any more news, Uan?" my Dad asked.

"Yes, when I reached Diving Board on my return, there were some Thai divers and a doctor with the boys. I think the doctor's going to remain with them. Other divers might come and stay at Diving Board with them. Still more divers might try to take the boys out using scuba equipment," I said.

"That's going to be a total disaster," my Dad said.

"After the first couple die doing that, they'll need to come up with another plan," Ton added.

"Maybe, but the divers seemed pretty confident," I said.

"Thai boys don't even know how to swim. Are they fucking aware of that?" Ton said.

"In their weakened condition the boys can't cave dive. That's a totally hair-brained idea!" my Dad said.

"Absurd!" Ton said.

"Just reporting what I heard. Don't shoot the messenger," I said.

"Earlier, you said on your return to Diving Board, did you go all the way up to the cave's entrance?" Ton asked with great concern.

"I went up as far as I could. There's a big international military contingent. It's growing. More international divers have joined the operation, too. The strong currents are preventing some of the rescuers from going deeper into the cave. I think they'll lay guidelines when they can get in there. Divers might be able to almost pull the boys through the cave.

"I believe that they were using pumps to pump water out of the cave, but accidentally may have pumped water back into another section of the cave," I said.

"So rather than diverting water from the cave, they flooded the cave by mistake?" my Dad asked.

"Maybe. That's probably why the passage under Upside-Down Shark's Fin flooded so rapidly. Bad timing for us," I said.

"Shit! How unlucky can you be? The timing …," Ton said.

"Either that or some of those holes that they drilled opened more flood gates," my Dad said.

"Terrible fucking timing!" Ton said.

"Look where we are. Nid and Uncle Moo both suffered from bad luck and bad timing throughout their entire lives," I said.

"Drowning is the worst way for a ghost to go," my Dad said.

"Other than by a monk!" Ton said.

I thought of the woman in the purple blouse, but I didn't mention her. She gave me some comfort. Although the two of us had never even spoken a single word, in an odd way, I used her to relieve my grief. I felt that I could share it with her.

"What can the rescuers do now to save the boys?" my Dad asked.

My Dad's question jarred me from my thoughts.

"It seems rather hopeless at the moment. They may be in a waiting game. There are many Thai Navy SEALs—strong, skilled, and fearless guys—prepping in the command-center area. I heard one SEAL diver being interviewed. I think he flew up from Bangkok. He stated that he won't rest until the boys are rescued," I said.

"I don't know how they'll get those boys out. Maybe they plan to feed and treat them in place, bring in oxygen, and get them out after monsoon season when the cave dries out," my Dad said.

"That's three months from now!" I said.

"I'll take care of them myself before then!" Ton said.

I still worried about crazy Ton.

"Imagine our headaches if they're around that long!" Ton added.

"If those boys all perish in our home, this place will be crawling with people after the monsoon season ends. Monks, too," my Dad said.

"Our home never will be the same," I said.

"We've passed that fucking point already!" Ton said.

"Yup," I agreed.

"Dammit!" Ton said.

"How much longer do you think those boys can hold on, Uan?" my Dad asked.

"One day. Maybe two, max. Not much more, unless the divers keep bringing them supplies," I said.

"Looks like we'll be getting a sacrifice soon," Ton said.

"Ton, how can you think about that now?" I said.

"We've already lost Nid and Moo today," my Dad said.

"I was born bad. My old man beat me before I became a hitman. I need to kill. It's in my nature," Ton said.

"It's in your nature? At least you're honest," I said.

"No. No, I'm not. But I am what I am," Ton declared.

What was that supposed to mean? Sick ghost.

My hatred for Ton built during the course of the past week. He had been a terrible person above ground, and he continued his ways in the subterranean. I couldn't believe that we shared common ancestors. I tried to block thoughts of me harming Ton, but my mind wouldn't clear of them.

I worried that Ton would take things into his own hands again. Two days ago he had been on the verge of committing a murder when the British cave divers appeared out of nowhere. Their timing had been magnificent. The loss of Nid and Moo weighed heavily on Ton. Although he didn't come right out and say it, Ton blamed the Wild Boars for their deaths. His hunger built to a crescendo.

I didn't know what to do. I needed time to think; I needed time to rest. If I blacked out during one of my round-trips, I wouldn't be able to serve the Wild Boars, to protect and help save them, to defend them against Ton, or to help my Dad when he needed me. Nid and Uncle Moo's deaths proved how dangerous traveling in the cave had become. Ghosts don't know how to swim either, and we never were meant to enter fast-moving water.

"Dad, I'm going to turn in now. I'm feeling really exhausted," I said.

Ton continued his drinking. My Dad hovered nearby.

"Okay, Uan. Sleep well. You did what you could today. It's not your fault. Get some rest now," my Dad said.

"Sure. Thanks, Dad. Good-night," I said.

I closed my eyes while thinking of the woman in the purple blouse. It felt great finally to have seen her again. I hoped to meet her again soon …

Chapter 21

I slept very little on the evening of July 4th. What a night. The image of the gorgeous woman in the purple blouse was quickly replaced by the image of my hand just missing Nid's wrist. Rather than experiencing satisfying dreams, my dreams tormented me. If Nid or I had reached in the opposite direction just a few inches, I might have saved him. Bad timing. The picture of his melting insides haunted me and made me sick to my stomach. While tossing and turning, I spit up a few times during the night.

I lost Uncle Moo, too. In my dreams I heard Uncle Moo burping over and over again. Losing an uncle didn't hurt as much as losing a brother, but it still upset me. In any case, there was nothing that I could have done for Uncle Moo. He disappeared before I knew it, but I'd come within a hair's breadth of saving poor Nid. Maybe the British cave divers who'd discovered the Wild Boars felt similarly to me. They'd come so close to saving the Wild Boars but couldn't quite complete the rescue, at least not yet.

When I finally climbed out of bed, I felt wrecked physically. My neck hurt like hell as did all my flying and climbing muscles. I lost a huge amount of weight over the past 12 days. Emotionally, the Wild Boar incident drained me. But despite my worsening condition and the grave dangers, I felt a great need to go on another recon.

"Morning, Dad."

"Morning, Uan."

"In spite of what happened yesterday, I'm planning to do my usual recon today," I said.

"That's a good idea, Uan," Ton said.

I could see a look of total concern on my Dad's face.

"Uan, use extra caution. I've got a bad feeling! I'm worried about you. The flood waters are rising. Even you might not be able to get through. Please don't take any unnecessary risks, son," my Dad said.

"Don't worry about me, Dad. I'll be careful. I promise," I said.

I felt concerned, though, especially after yesterday's drownings. Observing the Thai Navy SEALs somehow gave me the strength and courage to continue. When I watched the risks that the SEALs and volunteers willingly undertook, I became inspired to be part of the mission. The courage displayed by the Wild Boars also gave me courage.

"Remember, you're tired. Don't make any stupid decisions. Stop. Think. Act," my Dad admonished.

"Thanks, Dad. I'll use extreme caution. I'm going now," I said.

My Dad came over and gave me a big hug. He seemed troubled. Did he sense something? My Dad never had hugged me before any of my other recon missions. He flew over to his sentry position and folded his arms.

"Be careful, Uan," Ton said unexpectedly while patting me on the back.

The loss of Nid and Moo seemed to have had a calming influence on Ton. He suddenly acted more caring. Maybe part of it was that he no longer had supporters. He no longer held a majority. Or, was this just some sort of performance? I didn't trust Ton. He is a liar and an insane murderer.

"Thanks, Ton," I said while masking my doubts about his sincerity.

"Be careful, Uan," Ton repeated.

"I will," I said.

My Dad looked unsettled. Did he and Ton have an exchange this morning that I'd missed?

"Bye, Dad. Love you always!" I said.

"Good luck. Love you, too! See you later, Uan," my Dad said.

And, with my Dad's final words to me, I headed back toward Diving Board.

◆◆◆◆◆

What would July 5th bring? I made my way successfully back to Diving Board with no close calls. I
assumed the usual vantage point near my stalactite.
I watched as the doctor treated and fed the Wild
Boars in their confined space. Against all odds,
none of the Wild Boars had died yet. The conditions in my home were dreadful, dark, and damp.
To my amazement I watched some of the boys getting stronger through the doctor's efforts. I gripped
my stalactite.

I couldn't help but shake my head. How could
the Wild Boars manage to endure? The human spirit and encouragement from one another had kept
them going for 13 days. The initial contact from the
British cave divers probably had given them an
ounce of hope, and maybe all that they needed was
an ounce. But their prospects remained terribly
bleak. And I saw no signs that any divers would be
returning today.

Once again, the level of hardship that these
poor little boys endured became too much for me
to bear. I couldn't watch them anymore. I was a
mess. I remembered my Dad's advice about using
extreme caution today. In my current state I realized that I couldn't safely push on to Pattaya Beach
and beyond. I decided to retrace my steps. Play
things conservatively today.

On the return trip I said a prayer for the Wild Boars. I hoped that when I came back again, they would all still be alive. I thought of the woman in purple. She seemed to have cast a spell over me. I reflected about how I'd changed through my interactions with the Wild Boars and the cave divers. Having a cluttered mind somehow made my return passage go more quickly. I exercised caution despite my distracted mind and arrived safely.

I'd grown accustomed to meeting my Dad at his sentry position. When I returned early, I knew that he would breathe a big sigh of relief. Ton probably wouldn't be as happy to see me returning since I really didn't have anything much to report. He would be angry that I'd cut my reconnaissance mission short. Let him be mad. I just didn't feel up to a long journey today.

Chapter 22

When I came into view of my Dad's sentry post, it seemed strange that I didn't see him waiting there. I put my finger back down and immediately became worried. His last words to me were "See you later, Uan." Where was he? My mind raced. I flew quickly. Although it wouldn't be in Dad's character, I supposed that he was probably taking a break from his sentry duty. When I found him, I would tease him about leaving his post. Ha-ha.

When I rounded the bend, I saw my Dad on the cave's floor.

"Nooooooooooo! No, no, no, no, noooooo!" I screamed.

I shook violently and clenched my fists. Blood covered my Dad's body. Ton's knife protruded from his heart. I went berserk flying wildly. Ton, you fucking murderer! Where was he? What would I do now? Calm down, Uan. But I couldn't calm down. My Dad had just been murdered by my fucking cousin! I went insane.

"Nooooooo! Ton?"

Then I saw Ton. His hands covered in blood. He paced back and forth. I'm sure that he hadn't expected me to return this soon. I saw a crazed look in his eyes. He must have seen the same one in mine. Think, Uan. Think. Your Dad is gone, but you still can save the Wild Boars. I broke the stare-down's silence.

"Ton, what the fuck happened?"

"I tried to reason with him, Uan. He reached for my knife. I honestly had no choice."

"So you killed him. You killed my Dad."

"Like I said, Uan. I didn't have a choice. We argued …"

"Oh, fuck!"

Think, Uan. I remembered my Dad's advice: stop, think, and act. But there wasn't time. Come on, Uan. I had an idea—one as crazy as the wild scuba rescue of the Wild Boars. Ton never would anticipate such a plan; he never could have conceived of such a plan.

"Help me move his body, Ton. We can't leave him like this. Help me! Grab my Dad's feet, Ton!"

My raised voice and command startled Ton. In his shocked state Ton moved toward my Dad's feet.

"I'll grab his hands. Let's move him to that cubby."

Ton clutched my Dad by the ankles. I gripped his wrists.

"Ready to move him? Go. Lift up. Take him over there!"

I nodded in the direction of intended travel.

My nod gave me a split second in which to act. I dropped my Dad's head on the rocks, a move that Ton never would have suspected, and jerked the knife from my Dad's chest. I lunged at Ton's heart. In mid-air I placed my other hand over the heel of the knife and tightened my grip on its handle. I drove the blade deep into Ton's chest. I landed on him and felt his warm blood running between us. I had hit his heart.

"You fucker! I hate you! Release the Wild Boars! Release the Wild Boars!"

I pushed the knife in deeper and twisted with all my might. Kneeling now, I grabbed a handful of Ton's hair with my hand and, pulling upward with a mighty force, I swung the knife toward his neck. I heard a loud swish! I held Ton's severed head in my hand. I moved his blood-dripping face directly in front of mine.

I shouted, "You fucking jerk! You evil bastard!"

Ton never heard my cursing. He was dead. Decapitated. I took one more look at Ton's white face and then smashed it repeatedly against the cave's wall turning his features into a bloody pulp.

"Release the Wild Boars! Release the Wild Boars!"

My voice boomed through the dark chamber. As my echo dampened, I heard only the eerie, irregular pitter-patter of dripping water. No reply came. Flying around in a wild rage, I almost lost control. My back hit and broke off a small stalactite. Ouch!

Would my demand be enough? It needed to be for the sake of the Wild Boars. They couldn't hang on much longer.

Chapter 23

Poof.

"I'm the Sleeping Lady of the Mountain. Above ground I was a princess. This is my daughter Angie."

Poof. My Dad and Ton's bodies went up in smoke before my eyes. No trace remained. I hurriedly backed up. My God! Somehow saying "Pleased to meet you" didn't seem like a good idea. Where had they come from? Had she heard my appeal?

Angie was the woman in the purple blouse! I knew that I'd recognized her face. Angie is a ghost, too. She looked just like her mother—the lover of the man who Ton murdered centuries ago. I never had forgotten the princess's face.

"You've broken a terrible spell by killing your cousin. When Pet went into the hills that day so very many years ago, I followed him. We planned to elope, get married, and raise a family. To return only much later, once my father's grandchildren had grown up," the princess said.

"Pet?" I asked.

"Yes, the common man who was my lover," the princess said.

"My cousin was hired by your father to kill Pet?" I asked.

"Yes," the princess said.

The puzzle pieces began falling together.

"My cousin asked my father, me, my uncle, and my brother to accompany him on that unforgettable day. We really didn't know what we were getting into," I said.

"I never blamed you. You were the only one who cared about Pet. I never forgot that you made an effort to save him. I remember seeing your father restrain you," the princess said.

"My Dad tried to save my life. My cousin was an evil killer," I said.

"That's why my father hired him. After Pet's murder I had no reason to live. I took my own life, transformed into the Mountain of the Sleeping Lady, and trapped the five of you in my stomach. At the time I didn't know that I was pregnant, or I wouldn't have taken my own life. I gave birth to Angie underground," the princess said.

"She's never been outside the cave?" I asked.

"No, never! A ghost child who's born in a cave can never leave it," the princess explained.

"What about the Wild Boars?" I asked.

"Angie's been watching the World Cup that's taking place currently in Russia. She wants her own soccer team. Given the opportunity, she trapped the boys. Angie plans to keep them in the cave with her forever," the princess said.

"You've got to be fucking kidding me, right?" I asked.

"Mother knows that I want my own team," Angie said.

How could someone so lovely be so twisted? Hell, she had never been above ground. I couldn't believe what I was hearing. So it wasn't merely a coincidence that the Wild Boars were in the wrong place at the wrong time.

"Angie, those boys are completely innocent," I said.

"I don't care. I want my own team," Angie said.

WTF. Spoiled brat! Think, Uan. Think. Come on, come on!

"You're very beautiful, Angie," I said.

I paid Angie a compliment. Would it help? Was it the first compliment of her life? I continued.

"I understand your loneliness. I've been trapped here for centuries with no partner. Taking an entire soccer team into the underground isn't the solution though. You'd be killing a group of innocent boys. Taking them away from their families. Since you trapped them here, they've been struggling so hard to stay alive. They all have a strong will to live. The international community wants them to live," I said.

I was reaching. The situation was a total disaster. An absolute nightmare. Four ghosts already had died. Tham Luang Cave had been changed forever.

"What do you suggest, Uan? That's your name, right?" Angie asked.

"Yes," I said.

Had Angie seen me admiring her near the cave's entrance? How much did she know about me? She knew my name.

"You don't look fat," Angie said while blushing.

"I was once, not so long ago," I said.

"I've tried, but I can't talk any sense into her. She never listens to her mother. We've got a real problem on our hands, Uan. The cave is suffering. They've drilled holes all over me. Pumped my stomach. I'll never be the same," the princess said.

That was a great understatement. I tried to push a terrible recurring thought out of my mind—negotiate with a man's life. Angie probably wouldn't go for it anyway. Like the rescuers, I, too, had become obsessed with saving the Wild Boars. Sacrifice one man for the lives of 13. I couldn't bear the thought, but then involuntarily I blurted it out.

"Angie, I saw an extremely handsome Thai Navy SEAL. His name is SEA, at least that's what I call him," I said.

"So?" Angie said.

"You're lonely in here without a companion. You two would make a lovely couple. You're so pretty, Angie. Extremely beautiful. He's a great guy. I think that you easily could fall in love with him," I said.

Angie blushed again.

"He's right, Darling. You suffer from an overwhelming loneliness. You need a companion," the princess said.

"What do you expect, Momma. I was born in a cave," Angie said.

Angie's voice was hauntingly sweet. Her innocence from being sheltered in the cave was immense. Did she even know the meaning of right and wrong? If not, she wouldn't be able to comprehend their difference.

"It's not your fault, Darling. My father caused all this trouble—his horrible greed. In order to save face, he didn't want me to marry a common man. He never understood Pet's and my love. We were meant for each other, soulmates. We died for each other," the princess said.

"I never even met my father," Angie said.

"That's a terrible shame, Angie," I said.

I almost added to my statement, but instead paused.

"I'm sorry, Honey. He was a wonderful and kind man. In some ways you remind me of him," the princess said.

I tried to stop myself, but words just flowed out of my mouth.

"SEA is a wonderful man. I admire him greatly. He's articulate, smart, gentle, and athletic. He came here to rescue the boys that you trapped. I believe that he would trade his life for those of the Wild Boars and their assistant coach. He already has taken huge risks in diving through the murk to stage tanks for other divers. If he stayed in the cave, everyone would assume that it was an accident," I said.

"Would he love me?" Angie asked.

"Angie, you're beautiful," I said.

Angie blushed. On the outside Angie appeared stunningly beautiful, but on the inside she seemed naïve and childish. Had I lost my mind? What was I doing? I could only think of the Wild Boars and their assistant coach. I felt that I was under some sort of spell.

"On his next dive, Angie, you could take him with you. It'll look like he ran out of air. If he knew that the Wild Boars were all going to live, that would give him great joy! I believe that he would forgive you," I said.

I felt sick to my stomach. I admired SEA enormously. He was my hero. I had my back against the wall, though, with the princess and her daughter. When I asked myself the tough question of whether SEA would trade his life for those of the Wild Boars and their assistant coach, I kept coming up with the same answer: yes. Yes, SEA would. I felt sure of myself, but I couldn't speak for him.

SEA had been trained to serve others. When faced with such a difficult decision, I believed that he would have traded his life. SEA didn't want any personal recognition. He didn't want to be a hero. SEA just wanted to do what he considered his duty. He had the ability to help, so he did help. I knew that SEA's sacrifice would make him a national hero of Thailand, but that didn't console me in the least.

I started the unthinkable negotiation, but I couldn't stop it. I needed assurances.

"Will both of you promise me that all of the Wild Boars and their assistant coach will go free in exchange for Angie's taking a companion?" I asked.

"I promise," Angie said and held her hand over her heart.

"I promise," the princess mimicked her daughter.

"And that SEA's death will be made to look like a diving accident?" I asked.

"Yes, it will appear as if he suffocated from running out of air," Angie said.

"He won't feel any pain?" I asked.

"No, he'll go peacefully," Angie said.

I spit up and squeezed the back of my neck with both hands. The stress became too much. I thought about SEA's ultimate sacrifice. I truly believed, though, that given the choice, it was what he would have wanted. He's a great man.

"I also want you to promise me that no harm comes to anyone else who's on the scene. No other volunteers will be harmed. No one else will be taken," I said.

"Yes, I promise," Angie said.

"Me, too," the princess said.

"Okay, we're all agreed. We have a deal," I said.

I shook hands with the two ladies.

"Agreed," I said.

"Agreed," Angie said.

"Thank you, Uan. You're very brave," the princess said.

"Yes, this way is better, Uan. Let the Wild Boars and their assistant coach live. Thank you, Uan. Thanks for showing me another way," Angie said.

"You'll always be there for SEA?" I asked still second guessing myself.

"Yes, I'll take care of him from now on," Angie said.

"Please make sure that *all* of the Wild Boars get out of the cave safely," I said.

"We will, Uan. I promise. My mother and I will release the Wild Boars. They'll all be allowed to go free. The assistant coach and everyone else in the cave. No one else will be harmed," Angie said.

Although I felt absolutely terrible about SEA, I believed that the most favorable possible compromise had been reached. My heart broke, and I needed to cry. My emotions took over, but I couldn't cry in front of the princess and Angie. I needed to remain strong like SEA and the Wild Boars. Keep it together, Uan, I encouraged myself.

I reasoned that if the Wild Boars weren't released by the cave, many other volunteers might die in a futile and prolonged effort to save the boys. The Wild Boars themselves probably would all die. Even those thoughts gave me little comfort right now. The princess could tell how distraught I felt. I could see Angie's eyes dreaming about SEA and their future. She'd fallen in love with my description of SEA. The princess reached out her hand to me.

"Here, Uan, take these. You're going to need them where you're going," the princess said.

It was a pair of sunglasses. I reached out and took them from her hand. A tear rolled down my cheek.

"You're free to leave the cave now, Uan. You've been a good ghost and you'll be a good man. I have no need for you here any longer. The cave is releasing you. I'm releasing. Returning you above ground. You've helped us find a solution to this unpleasant problem. You've saved many lives," the princess said.

"Thanks, princess," I said.

"Good luck, Uan. Thanks for what you've done for me," Angie said.

I got choked up.

"Thanks, Angie," I said.

"Good-bye, Uan," the princess said.

"Good-bye," Angie said.

"Good-bye," I said.

And then, just like that, poof, the princess and Angie disappeared from my life forever.

Chapter 24

A hand firmly grabbed my wrist, as I cleared the cave's entrance for the first time in hundreds of years. The wrinkled hand's vice-like grip forced me to stop.

"Who are you?" an old, deep voice demanded to know.

I looked down through my dark sunglasses and saw an orange robe. My heart raced. Remain calm, Uan. You've got this.

"Just another volunteer helping out with the rescue of the Wild Boars from Moo Pa Academy," I said.

"Not with milky-white skin like that you're not. What's in the bag?"

"It's full of money," I said.

I'd stuffed the bag with all of the cash that we'd accumulated over the years, and I thought it best not to lie to the Orange.

"Go! Go now before I change my mind. Thank you. Thank you for what you've done here. The princess and her daughter are at peace again.

You've been a great help in minimizing the loss of life. In releasing the Wild Boars."

The Orange somehow seemed to be aware of everything that had transpired in the cave. The monk didn't have to tell me to go a second time. In the cave over the past two weeks, I learned that timing was everything. I walked briskly with my back toward the cave's entrance. A burning sensation permeated my foreman. The pain caused from being touched by the monk gradually subsided. His positive feedback put my mind a bit more at ease.

The sun on my face felt good. The fresh air filled my lungs. Even with the sunglasses covering my eyes, I needed to squint. Reporters of many nationalities ran around helter-skelter with their notebooks and dangling cameras cornering and questioning dozens of people about their impressions of the incident. Everyone, except me, speculated as to whether or not the Wild Boars and their assistant coach would be rescued successfully. I needed to get away from this media circus.

In the news I learned later that a Thai Navy SEAL, named Samarn Gunan, had died around 1:00 a.m. on the morning of July 6th. Was he SEA? Angie hadn't wasted any time. The Internet stories reported that the Thai Navy SEAL drowned while staging tanks. Although his dive buddy had tried to revive his partner, the Navy SEAL died of suffocation. I felt deeply troubled about the loss of life. I hoped and prayed that the princess and Angie were satisfied, and that there wouldn't be any more trouble in the cave.

I followed the remainder of the story of the daring rescue of the Wild Boars and their assistant coach even though I already knew the outcome. On July 10th, 18 days after Angie began this ordeal, the final four boys and their assistant coach were safe. The bold mission had been executed to perfection.

The three Thai Navy SEALs and the Thai doctor who had remained at Diving Board with the boys at the tail end of the rescue mission came out of the cave safely, too. The princess and Angie had kept their promises, as the monk had intimated when I was allowed to pass. For that, I felt extremely happy. I knew that the cave was in good hands now.

Samarn Gunan was given a much-deserved national royal Thai cremation ceremony to celebrate his extraordinary life, heroism, and courage. He posthumously received a promotion of seven ranks to lieutenant commander. Although Lieutenant Commander Gunan wouldn't have wanted any recognition for himself, it was a beautiful gesture for his family, friends, and all of Thailand.

Samarn quickly became an international hero. I continue to admire his extraordinary bravery, devotion, and self-sacrifice in the name of service to others. He was a great man. Whenever I think of Samarn, I become very emotional.

Although the Wild Boars were invited to the FIFA World Cup finals in Russia, they weren't strong enough yet to travel and couldn't even watch the game live. I suspected by the time next season rolls around they would be able to accept the invitation which they received to watch Manchester United play at Old Trafford. I hoped that they would be able to return to the soccer field themselves soon.

I hoped that the Wild Boars would go on to dream big and chase those dreams with great passion. So many gave so much so they would have a second chance. Uncle Moo, my brother Nid, my Dad, my cousin Ton, and I had spent most of our lives linked together by a single event. I knew that forever-more the boys of Tham Luang Cave in the Mountain of the Sleeping Lady would be linked together in a similar way—an unbreakable bond formed out of necessity in the name of survival. I knew that they, too, would think of Lieutenant Commander Gunan often.

Tham Luang Cave would never be the same. After the Wild Boars were rescued, I felt sure that the place would be turned into a living museum—one that documented the brave and courageous international rescue mission and remembered Lieutenant Commander Gunan for the great hero that he was. Thai people are fantastic entrepreneurs. Would there be a movie? I felt certain that one was being created already. Would I go watch it? Probably, why not? No one in the above-ground world would ever know the role that I played during the ordeal.

◆ ◆ ◆ ◆ ◆

After a few weeks in Bangkok, I caught up on all the R&R that I'd missed out on over the last few centuries. With my huge bagful of cash just a bit lighter, I decided to head for Palm Springs. I wanted to spend the rest of my days in the sunniest place on the planet. Maybe buy a house there. Relax out on my deck while eating chips and guacamole, sipping Dos Equis, and listening to the Beach Boys. I knew that I would continue to think of Lieutenant Commander Gunan often. I hoped that he forgave me. He is my hero and inspiration.

I headed for California in search of a sunny life and a soulmate to share it with …

BOOKS BY RAYMOND GREENLAW

PALMARÈS (also available in electronic form).

The Thai Wife Story JOY (also available in electronic form), Book 1 of *The Thai Wife Series of Novels.*

The Thai Wife Story STAR (also available in electronic form), Book 2 of *The Thai Wife Series of Novels.*

Raymond's Checklist for Traveling in the USA (also available in electronic form), Book 1 of *Raymond's Checklist Series.*

Raymond's Checklist for Traveling in Thailand (also available in electronic form), Book 2 of *Raymond's Checklist Series.*

Raymond's Checklist for Traveling the World (also available in electronic form), Book 3 of *Raymond's Checklist Series.*

Raymond's Checklist for His Personal Bucket List (also available in electronic form), Book 4 of *Raymond's Checklist Series.*

Raymond's Checklist for Gear for a Long Hike (also available in electronic form), Book 5 of *Raymond's Checklist Series.*

Raymond's Checklist Cycling Gear (also available in electronic form), Book 6 of *Raymond's Checklist Series*.

The Hazards of Cycling in Thailand: Guidelines for Tourists (also available in electronic form).

Trapped in Thailand's Cave (also available in electronic form).

The Pacific Crest Trail: Its Fastest Hike, second edition (also available in electronic form).

Bob: My Dad, the Fisherman: A Father and Son's Relationship (also available in electronic form).

(With Saowaluk Rattanaudomsawat) *Essential Conversational Thai: Learn to Speak Thai Quickly, while Traveling in Thailand.*

You'll Never Walk Alone: Love Poems for My Sweetheart (also available in electronic form).

Poems of Raymond Greenlaw, 1986–2005 (also available in electronic form).

The Fastest Hike across Thailand (expected December 2021).

ABOUT THE AUTHOR

Raymond "Wall" Greenlaw was born in Providence, Rhode Island, USA to Roxy and Bob. Raymond has always enjoyed nature, big trees, lakes, mountains, and the sea. He writes about a wide range of topics and is the author of 35+ books.